Raymond Crane

The Secret Journals of Alien X

AF205024

Raymond Crane

The Secret Journals of Alien X

A Novella

JustFiction Edition

Impressum/Imprint (nur für Deutschland/only for Germany)
Bibliografische Information der Deutschen Nationalbibliothek: Die Deutsche Nationalbibliothek verzeichnet diese Publikation in der Deutschen Nationalbibliografie; detaillierte bibliografische Daten sind im Internet über http://dnb.d-nb.de abrufbar.
Alle in diesem Buch genannten Marken und Produktnamen unterliegen warenzeichen-, marken- oder patentrechtlichem Schutz bzw. sind Warenzeichen oder eingetragene Warenzeichen der jeweiligen Inhaber. Die Wiedergabe von Marken, Produktnamen, Gebrauchsnamen, Handelsnamen, Warenbezeichnungen u.s.w. in diesem Werk berechtigt auch ohne besondere Kennzeichnung nicht zu der Annahme, dass solche Namen im Sinne der Warenzeichen- und Markenschutzgesetzgebung als frei zu betrachten wären und daher von jedermann benutzt werden dürften.

Coverbild: www.ingimage.com

Verlag: JustFiction! Edition ist ein Imprint der
LAP LAMBERT Academic Publishing GmbH & Co. KG
Heinrich-Böcking-Str. 6-8, 66121 Saarbrücken, Deutschland
Telefon +49 681 37 20 310, Telefax +49 681 37 20 310-9
Email: info@justfiction-edition.com

Herstellung in Deutschland:
Schaltungsdienst Lange o.H.G., Berlin
Books on Demand GmbH, Norderstedt
Reha GmbH, Saarbrücken
Amazon Distribution GmbH, Leipzig
ISBN: 978-3-8454-4560-1

Imprint (only for USA, GB)
Bibliographic information published by the Deutsche Nationalbibliothek: The Deutsche Nationalbibliothek lists this publication in the Deutsche Nationalbibliografie; detailed bibliographic data are available in the Internet at http://dnb.d-nb.de.
Any brand names and product names mentioned in this book are subject to trademark, brand or patent protection and are trademarks or registered trademarks of their respective holders. The use of brand names, product names, common names, trade names, product descriptions etc. even without a particular marking in this works is in no way to be construed to mean that such names may be regarded as unrestricted in respect of trademark and brand protection legislation and could thus be used by anyone.

Cover image: www.ingimage.com

Publisher: JustFiction! Edition
is an imprint of the publishing house
LAP LAMBERT Academic Publishing GmbH & Co. KG
Heinrich-Böcking-Str. 6-8, 66121 Saarbrücken, Germany
Phone +49 681 37 20 310, Fax +49 681 37 20 310-9
Email: info@justfiction-edition.com

Printed in the U.S.A.
Printed in the U.K. by (see last page)
ISBN: 978-3-8454-4560-1

PART I

The Dreams that Things are Made of

Firstly, I must take this opportunity to say how insignificant I feel as a visitor to planet Earth.

The reader may realise during the course of reading the following account that my use of Earth language is simple, even meagre, for the purpose of describing the experiences that happened to me, and because of me. Remember I have no memory of the time before I came to earth, I have only a sketchy outline of the vocabulary so that even an earthchild could express their feelings better than I.

I must also heartily thank Mrs. Miriam Bilder for her co-operation and collaboration, and also her husband for the intrusive utilization of his body and soul. I can only hope that he can by now bring it upon himself to forgive me and to see that all the while I only meant to fulfil his dreams.

Summer 2023
Alien X

I hear birds, morning birds, the birds of earth. I have awoken; now to realize where and who I am.

I am lying horizontally, as humans do when they sleep. I feel the extremities of my human body, my head, my hands, my feet. I am lying in a bed in a darkened room. The bed is warm. There is someone next to me. I know it is my earthly wife. I know that I have arrived. Now to confront a human being; my first meeting with a being from another part of the universe.

I will have to explain to her when she awakens that I am an alien inhabiting her husband's body; a body; a life chosen because it is quite healthy, quite normal and a life from which I can learn the ways of earthlings.

She moves. Now I will have to speak for the first time as an earthling. She's first: "Mmmmn Good morning."

"Good morning." Does she know?

"Ahh, it's so good knowing you have holidays for the next two weeks."

"Holidays? Yes holidays, it's good."

"We'll be free as birds."

"As birds, yes, right."

She sits up in bed. He sits up.

"So we can take the kids to Stockhaven."

"The kids, Stockhaven, yes, right."

"Listen I have something to tell you," I said.

"OK."

"I'm an alien."

"You're a…a…an alien..*alien*?"

"Yes I am inhabiting your husband's body."

"His body? …Are you for real?"

"Yes, it's true."

"Since when?"

"Since this morning."

"Oh? Just like that? You're an alien."

"Yes."

"OK, I'll play along - so where are you from Mr. Alien?"

"A solar system far from Earth."

"And what are you doing..ah..in my husband's body?"

"I am here to learn the ways of earthlings."

"Ha! Ha! And for how long?"

"Until I am called back..home."

"Oh! Just like that. Yeh. Come on, the jokes gone far enough. Be real now."

"I am real, a real alien. I don't want to alarm you; I'm harmless, and I'll try to be just the same as your husband. I have his manners of speech but not his memory."

"What rubbish! Now tell me true, are we going to Stockhaven?"

"Sure anything you say. I have to become familiar with being a human and I don't want to be the cause of any distress on your part."

So this is how it went. I followed my wife into the bathroom and had a shower just as she had done. I went to the wardrobe as she did and selected some clothes. I dressed. We didn't say anything until downstairs at breakfast. She said, "So what you want for breakfast crazy Alien?"

"Same as usual thanks."

"Say, you had me worried for a while and even now you seem a little unsure of yourself."

"You would be too if it was your first day on earth."

"Oh! Come on, quit that! Or explain to me what you're on about this morning."

"Just like I said, I have come to learn the ways of earthlings and like the moon of earth eclipsing the sun I have eclipsed your husband's personality. I, an alien, am now he, your husband."

"Why! Why my husband out of billions? Is this an invasion, a body snatchers type of thing or what? Explain yourself now!"

"Your husband was chosen because he is healthy and normal and provides a good example of the average earthling's life. I can learn a lot."

"I say, just like that, Yeh! And you want me to carry on as usual I suppose."

"Yes, it won't be too much to endure, and I'll be cheerful about it."

"So we just go to Stockhaven with the kids as usual?"

"You'll have to explain that. Kids? Stockhaven?"

"We have two children, you know, and we always go to the mountains for the September holidays."

"So, OK, yes, Stockhaven it is..and by the way what are our children's names?"

"Why, you ignoramus, they're Sojosafao we call him Spin and Siriona people call her Siri."

"And please, please pardon my ignorance, what is your name?"

"Ah! Miriam."

"And, please pardon me, what is my name?"

"Oh! Randolph, Randolph Bilder."

"I realize that this is quite an inconvenience for you; I'm sorry about that, but we aliens have to learn somehow, sometime. We have so much to gain and you humans do too when we formally introduce ourselves."

"Yes well, what about my husband, what about Randy?"

"He'll be fine, physically and mentally; he just won't know what has happened when I leave his body. And it's like me, I don't remember anything before this morning, just some ground rules; like I should know some days before I leave that I'm going so I can tell you when it's time for me to go. "

"Ahh! It's a bit much to accept. How long will it be for? "

"Maybe years, what year is it by the way?"

"Ah! This could get tedious. It's 2023. And what am I supposed to call you, you know, what's your name?"

"I have no name that can be expressed in earth language; please, Miriam, call me Randolph or like you call your husband, just Randy. Please, OK? OK? "

"OK"

2

That afternoon we decided that I should have some driving lessons, learn to drive an earth vehicle. Firstly I studied the rules of the road for two hours and then we took a drive out of town. I learn very quickly; it was an automatic car and soon I could drive as well as Miriam's husband. I was ready for our trip to Stockhaven.

We picked up Spin and Siri from Miriam's mother's house. Her name I learnt is Dorothy and she accepted me on face sight quite normally it seemed to me. I am handling things very well and Miriam had apparently gotten used to me asking the odd question. We appear to be the perfect family; no one would guess that the father in this family is in fact an extra-terrestrial.

I was amazed at Spin and Siri. They were like small versions of us. Spin looked exactly like me and Siri looked just the same as Miriam. I drove for three hours; the trip to Stockhaven takes a whole day; then I changed places with Miriam. It was great sitting in the passenger seat of an earth car speeding on the auto way, the slip-stream of air riffling back my hair. I just wanted this feeling to go on forever. I know who I am and I am happy to be Randolph or Randy or dad or whatever. This quality, this ability to feel happiness, real contentment was what I was sent here to experience: to encode the sensations, to know in the recesses of my psychic make-up the fibre of living as a human. I am meant to know, to experience all the normal feelings of a human, not to do anything unusual or in any way super human. Challenges awaited me but I was already feeling grateful to the real Randolph Bilder. I wanted him to feel that he had gained a little of my values or in some way to demonstrate that with my help he could achieve something lasting from this intrusion into his everyday fulfilment, something I was coming to value highly. The winds of air as the car breezed this way, that way and straight forward seemed to blow the top off my head; yes, I was extremely light-headed and filled with happiness. Oh so being human has true joys; I felt a little reluctant to think that at any time the signal could come and I would have to depart, back to I couldn't remember where.

3

We rounded the cliffs after a long rise of highway into the mountains. The air was fresh and cool. Below us was the small town of Stockhaven and rising on all sides were mountains covered in white stuff. " What is that white stuff? " I exclaimed excitedly.

"Snow silly!" said Siri exasperatedly.

"And what is snow? " I quizzed her.

"It's frozen water that falls from the sky, silly one," cried Siri.

"You have seen it many times before," said Miriam as she pulled into the car park of a three storey building, "and this is the chalet where we stay every year."

When we were warm and settled inside the chalet I questioned Miriam as to how long we would be at Stockhaven and what we would be doing there.

"We will be here for one week only; that's usually enough time to relax and ski, and for Spin and Siri to play in the snow, "she said. "And what is *ski*, pray tell? " I asked.

"'Pray tell' - I like that, very Randyish. Just wait and see - it's great fun to ski and Randy was a very good skier."

So that was how it went. I learnt to glide down the slopes of the mountains over this..snow. I found my co-ordination was in amazingly good form. We skied every morning while the children played and walked round the town. Miriam was a very good skier too; she had more confidence than me and moved very gracefully, I thought. The week passed before I had time to think anything about my future; the hours were packed with throwing snowballs and what the kids liked the most, a thing called tobogganing.

Then we drove back along the auto-way stopping at cafes and restaurants - I found I had a great appetite and enjoyed everything we had to eat. It was a totally new experience for me, always something new to eat; new tastes, new textures; yes, I was going to enjoy this part of life, I could tell.

4

I took the initiative when we had returned from Stockhaven to ask some in-depth questions of Miriam. I wanted to know more of Randolph Bilder, just who did she think he is? Oh! Yes and who will I have to live up to; what relations will I as Randolph have with others. Miriam was more than enthusiastic to talk at length about her husband. Apparently and I had no reason or inclination not to believe her, they had married young, had been teenage sweethearts. That meant, so I was to learn, that Miriam and Randolph had a natural liking for each other, a mutual fondness from the first days of their introduction to each other.

Life was easy for them once they decided to get married, that meant; now I'm thinking, am I wearing my readers out with boring particulars. Anyway who am I addressing in this my account of my time on earth. Well it's mainly for Randolph to read when I am gone. Just so he will be aware that I acted with integrity and played his part as he would have wished, had he a say in the matter of my occupation of his position, his very soul.

Yes Randolph I wish to live your life just as you would have done.

There it is, they were married well that's normal and Randolph finished college and received a postgraduate degree in engineering. Then he got this job with the City Design Office where he has been ever since. Randolph worked hard and was promoted to the position of Landscape Architect. He had to study more and this he liked; he liked learning how things worked and putting materials to good use in the public domain where he found ample challenges for his expanding skills.

Miriam had supported him through University working in a florist shop in the city centre. When he had gotten his job she became a housewife full time and they started the process of building a family. This was the story of the Bilder family and Miriam had been eager to tell it like oral history or the adventures of Miriam and Randolph.

As time went by, Spin and Siri finally convinced them that they were adults capable of all that could possibly and normally be expected of any earthling who follows the natural thread of life continuing down through the ages to the present when, and she looked at me directly and searchingly, an alien took the place of her husband and she laughed absurdly, harshly as if with a heartfelt longing that normality should forever reign in the Bilder family.

I was a little shocked to see this show of emotion but I know it's real and that I am an intruder. Now I felt a desire to be gone, to go back to my known world and leave Miriam and Randolph to be themselves.

I have to know about this work Randolph does at the City Design Office. I will have to fill his place there next week. The sooner I experience the basic role of a human the sooner I will be called back home and things can return to the way they were.

I said to Miriam and I meant it, I was nearly crying .. a notion of my obligation was heavy upon me, I said that I would try and do something for Randolph. I wanted to leave earth a better place than when I came here. Somehow, someway I would reward Randolph and through Randolph the whole of humanity. Oh! I had grandiose hopes but as it will be seen the challenges of an average human are a good match for any extra-terrestrial.

5

My talks with Miriam during the next week revealed to me much about how a human being gains fulfilment in life. It seemed not too much to expect that I could add to the store of Randolph's achievements. Of course I had little idea when I might have to be going so I felt that the factor of time was imperative for me to do something worthwhile.

As I was to learn it is through Randolph's employment that I held the greatest hope of contributing to the life that now compelled me as if Randolph had been expecting me and prepared the way for a great leap forward.

Miriam told me that Randolph had been involved in a number of projects. He had designed a bridge, the Putney Bridge, named after the Design Office manager, Ralf Putney. It was a unique bridge made entirely of iron, and built to last forever. He had had a furnace constructed at the site and filled a mould with molten iron. By this project the manager was honoured so much that he had given other projects into the hands of Randolph. There was the giant chrome crab restaurant at Peekers Point, the Space Observatory with the kaleidoscopic lens that makes the stars dance. Randolph had come a long way since he started drawing up plans for public toilets and similar works.

I now felt sure that I could do something wonderful with this life. During the course of the week Miriam kept my body busy with some household chores. I had a long list of things to do to, make myself useful, as Miriam said. I had to cook, or wash the dishes; clean the floors, put out the rubbish and defrost the fridge. These things Randolph had regularly done to keep the household running smoothly.

One morning as I was defrosting the fridge I said to Siri, "But how did this snow fall out of the sky and into the fridge? "

Said Siri, "That's not snow that's frost! "

"But you said that snow was frozen water. "

"Yes," laughed Siri, "but when it's in the fridge it hasn't fallen from the sky it's just so cold in there that the water freezes. "

Well that caused a laugh in the family and the children thought I was just making a joke.

On the final day of my holidays Miriam gave me a briefing about the people I would be associating with at the Design Office. She showed me photos of everyone especially Ralf Putney and a man called Rex Gonzalez who was my assistant in the Landscape Architects office.

I now felt ready for the next stage of my great adventure.

6

On the last night of my holidays the family were together in the living room. Unexpectedly Spin said rather excitedly,

"What if I was to try marijuana?"

"Why would you want to do that?" said Miriam. "Isn't puberty enough? "

"Some boys were smoking it in the change rooms and I got a strong whiff of the stuff. It made me feel very happy," said Spin.

"So how does it affect you physically and mentally?" I said.

"It expands my mind by heightening perceptions," said Spin.

"Well look at me," I said. "I've never tried marijuana, have I Miriam?"

"Not that I am aware of," said Miriam.

"And am I not a good example of a human being?" said I.

"A fine role model," said Miriam.

"Yes" said Spin "and you designed the Putney Bridge and the Chrome Crab and the Space Observatory, and I know you're always happy."

"So what need is there for drugs?" said Miriam.

"None I suppose" said Spin "unless one day I become an artist."

I tried to think fast, I did not wish to reveal for Randolph's sake how much of a silly ignoramus I was so I did not allow Spin to be aware that I had no idea what an artist is.

"An artist may need an expanded mind but until you're an artist you may find an expanded mind a burden. If and when that day comes to pass it will then be your decision, your future," I said, trying to be very serious and responsible.

7

It was a hot Spring morning as I eased out of the drive-way of our house through the curving treed streets of this outer suburb and onto the auto way. Yes my days as Randolph the commuter are beginning, my first day of work at the City Design Office. I had listened to some earth music on the radio at home but as I saw a music playing machine in the car I selected a disc from about five that were under the front inside part of the car. I read the name .. Diana Kraul, an old disc I supposed by earth standards .. 2002 was written on the front. I poked it into the slot and pressed the play button.

Suddenly I seemed to be on another level, a whole new environment and the roadway streamed out before me, I accelerated. When Diana sings .. "I need you in my arms, "does she mean me, Randolph Bilder husband of Miriam, and yet to know what it's like to be held by someone .."hold close to the one who loves you," sang Diana.

Time drifts and I don't mind waiting at these flashing lights .. red, orange, green .. go! And waiting in the long line of cars that are all moving towards the city centre.

I know where the Design Office is, it's like some deep programmed part of me, as though I too am on automatic mode. I glide down, down under a very tall office building and park the car with hundreds of others.

8

I step out of this box which has taken me to the fifteenth floor of the office building. It is spacious up here with desks here and there, lots of light flooding in large windows. I notice that all the men are wearing suits and ties like me, some kind of costume for the working people I supposed. I pass along doors with names and titles written on them. I came to a door that has on it a bold, neat sign:

Randolph Bilder
Landscape Architect

I knock, no answer, I enter. There are three rooms, one has some machines; I don't know what they could be. The room on the right is larger; through the open door I see a large desk and several chairs. There is a large window through which I can see only sky and clouds, as I walk around the desk I see a photo of Miriam there, smiling. I say, hello Miriam.

On the walls of this room are photos of various buildings, some odd in appearance and titled The Putney Bridge, The Chrome Crab and the Starfinder Observatory. I surmise, Yes this is my office, my space; this is where I will plan the elevation of Randolph Bilder, designer extraordinaire.

After an hour of contemplation of my surroundings the outer door is opened and in steps a young man whom I recognize as being Rex Gonzalez my assistant.

"Good morning Randolph."

"Good morning Rex."

"And how were your holidays?"

"Fine thanks, Yes just fine."

"Did you manage to shoot a few holes at the club?"

"Er, shoot a few holes; well actually the family went to Stockhaven for some skiing."

"Oh yes of course, you do that every year. Say is it as good as they say."

"Oh yes better than they say. It is wonderful for the whole family. We really enjoyed it. I liked the trip especially, driving you know."

"Yes, and how is Miriam?"

"Very well thanks."

"By the way Ralf told me to leave these books and magazines for you; something about a new project." He placed a number of books on my desk.

"I have some to look at too that he has given me so I'll take the rest of the morning to see to that. You always said that fifty percent of this job is study, study and research, well I'm sure you're right, the computer does most of the hard work."

"OK Rex, I'll have a look at them, thanks," I said.

"Oh also, Ralf wants to see you in his office at 2 o'clock," said Rex.

"Yeh, OK. Thanks again Rex," I said.

Rex stepped lightly and silently on the thick carpet and disappeared into the other room. His office I assume it to be.

9

Randolph settled down upon his plush padded chair and drew the books and magazines towards him. One by one he perused the technical articles; he read about new materials for building, new materials for which no use had yet been thought of. He saw how research was going on steadily, surely by hundreds of research teams around the planet. His mind began to vibrate with an energy; inspired, and eager to apply this new technology.

A few hours passed as Randolph pondered and absorbed the new ideas and theories that he felt were going to make the name of Randolph Bilder famous on this planet, this planet potent with wonders and filled with the enthusiasm of science harnessed to create dreams; the dreams that things are made of.

Randolph stood and stretched. He felt that he was on the verge of creating something that could only be rivalled by nature, that melting pot of random power that was the source of all dreams.

He turned and looked out of his window and there was a sight he knew he would never forget as long as he was Randolph with the breath of life strong within him. It was a rainbow arching upwards and through the clouds; and there above the cloud bank the curve of colours magnificent in form, perfect in structure. Something will come of this, he thought.

Several hours later Rex entered his office.

"Find anything interesting?" said Rex.

"Yes well it's all interesting but some research is definitely useful for building large outdoor structures and as that is my specialty I would like you to search further, particularly this stuff being done in Uzbekistan; the boron, mercury crystals that are being used to build large housing estates. If you could check the most recent research and get back to me later; here I have made a note of the reference details."

"Yes OK, and I have found an interesting article about micro-lasers, nobody seems to know what to do with them yet. But I feel they have potential if we want to levitate a large structure or create something totally new and spectacular."

"Good work Rex, OK then, I'll head off to Ralf's office. Thanks and I'll see you before I go this evening."

10

I was stepping out of my office and heading down a wide corridor when a woman came out of one of the offices. She walked in front of me, she was about my age, my height, black haired, and seemed to walk with an especially lilting step, different from other people, other women. My eyes followed the movement of her body from legs to bottom to thin waist to slim back and then again to that long mane of black hair. It was like music, the way she moved, and Diana Kraul's song came into my head; "Hold me close, hold me tight."

When we came to the end of the corridor we reached a door which had written on it in large letters:

RALF PUTNEY
CITY DESIGN MANAGER

The woman knocked quietly and entered, I looked at my watch, it was exactly 2 o'clock. The woman left the door open for me, and as she turned I caught a glimpse of her face. It was like magic; something familiar and thrilling in the eyes, something elegant in the nose and mouth. I was stunned at this new feeling, I knew it was a male, female attraction thing, a very common feeling that all humans have. I followed her through a large outer office where a woman sat at a large desk, talking on the phone. The woman that was ahead of me opened a large door and entered another room, closing the door behind her, I waited at the desk, I felt a sense of premonition, that a new challenge was awaiting me in that room where the woman had entered, leaving me feeling apprehensive, shook up and thinking , is this normal.

'Randolph, 'I said to myself, 'you must accept yourself, accept your feelings; just be natural, and don't let being a human preoccupy you; yes, just be prepared to do your job whatever that may entail. '

11

At first I was surprised by the size of the room, it was three times the size of my office and the thing about it that immediately caused a sensation of floating was that the three walls opposite the door and the ceiling were made of clear glass. I was floating in the sky, blue and clouded, with light permeating every corner, no shadows. It was a wonderful feeling. I must have been here before I thought, the room seemed to have a place in my psyche; like the rainbow, it filled me with wonder.

Then I saw a man standing near a large chair, and on the chair sat the woman, the woman who had aroused those feelings in me, from a hidden and undiscovered part of me. I must have been staring at her because the man made a noise; cleared his throat. He had been turned away from me towards the woman but now he moved around to the other side of her chair and looked intently in my direction. It was Ralf, Ralf Putney, a man of approximately sixty years of age with a greying patchy beard and a smile that matched his words,

"Hi Randolph, how are you today? "

"Very well thanks Ralf or should I call you Mr. Putney? "

"Oh you know me and anyone that the public relations department doesn't know calls me Mr. Putney but you Randolph have always called me Ralf. So be it, and this of course is Shiree, you know each other. "

"Good afternoon," exclaimed Shiree her voice lilting like a familiar melody.

"Oh, good afternoon to you Shiree," I said, wondering just how familiar Randolph had been with this vivacious woman who seemed to be sitting on a cloud.

"Well usually it's Mrs. Putney to you, " said Ralf, "but today I want to talk with you about something rather personal. We'll talk about the new project later. "

"I have a proposition for you," he said smiling, he seemed very happy and very sure of himself. "Just something I want you to consider very seriously," and he glanced at Shiree. She was smiling at me. It felt very good, this familiarity that seemed to hint of something more.

"I am sixty-three this year. I'm not getting any younger. Soon I will be retiring and someone will take my place as manager of the City Design Office, consider that.

I know you well Randolph. I've seen you rise from humble beginnings until now, today, you seem fit to achieve real significance in your career. You have always been a strong family man, a devoted husband and we have always gotten along very, very well. In fact Randolph you know me better than most and I know you almost like a brother. We have been very friendly over the years. And another thing you know Shiree rather well; well, well enough. "

There was a short silence, he was glancing at Shiree and then back to me. She kept smiling, there was something unusual about her face, her eyes rather angular and oval shaped and her skin was like a golden pearl. Maybe, I thought she is not a native of these parts of this particular part of the world.

"The thing is, Randolph, I am unable to have a child, the male menopause you understand. And Shiree here, would very much like to have a child. We can't do it together Randolph; Shiree and I can not make a baby, God knows we've tried."

He paused again and walked on that thick carpet that made not a sound as clouds wafted around him and Shiree.

"What I am suggesting Randolph is that you kind of intercede on my behalf and give us a little help. Kind of let nature take it's course. I have noticed that you do not find Shiree unattractive and you are both quite healthy. It's just a little delicate to ask this of you but," he paused again and raised an eyebrow, " tell me, if you don't mind Randolph , how's your sex-life with Miriam? "

"Honestly I don't know, I mean I don't remember." I was out of my depth.

He raised his eyebrows and cleared his throat again, "Not good, eh?,"

"Listen Randolph, I'm stuck; I don't know what else to do, and I don't know who else to trust." He gave me a great smile, stepped over to me, putting his arm around my shoulders and bringing his face close to mine, he winked. "It'll be alright, you'll see!"

I was far from being prepared for such an unexpected proposal. I was blinking out into the clouds not knowing what to say or do next. Eventually Ralf stood apart from me and strode, with a sense of having relieved a great weight from his conscience, over to the far window. He stood looking out of the window with his hands clasped behind his back.

I was still blinking into the distance and Ralf, his stature always apparent, seemed to be not an obstacle but a door to the sky; to some future that would not have occurred I'm sure even in Randolph's sanest dreams.

Without a thought I became aware that I was staring at Shiree again. She was still smiling, so still, so patient, so ... and she rose from her chair like a sleek and subtle expression of something deep within me. She came towards me, she looked straight into my eyes and said quite unruffled, quite breezily --- "Taboo or not taboo that is the question!" She was very softly spoken and I could smell a sweet intoxicating fragrance. "Give of yourself," she whispered.

"Is this normal?" I said rather stunned by her presence.

"Very normal but also a little unusual," she said, "but one night with me and you won't regret it will you? Miriam need never know; they say what one doesn't know can never hurt one."

As I looked passed those eyes that seemed to glow with earthly wisdom I heard an inner voice singing, "Hold me tonight as though this night could never end." It was the words of that Diana Kraul song and they made sense to me.

"We will have to see about that," I said, "certainly your offer has it's merits and I would of course like to do you and Ralf any favour that I can. At the moment the proposal will require some further consideration. I hope that you and Ralf can bear with me while I think it over for a few days. Is that OK?"

"You should feel honoured, it's an extreme circumstance that needs extreme and not unnatural strength on your part and I must say that I find you quite suitable for the purpose." Shiree paused. "What you feel is important too, so yes take a few days; I'll be waiting."

Shiree turned, the room span in a dizzying swirl as she returned to her chair. The silent clouds danced a merry dance and Shiree smiled; "magic," thought I as Ralf turned and quickly moved the conversation on to tomorrow.

"I'll expect to see you at the golf club tomorrow at 2 o'clock. We'll talk about this new project then. Business as usual hey sport!"

Ralf smiled, stepped over to me and held out his hand. I accepted his handshake with a sense that I should not forget formalities, I was even glad. I took one more quick glance at Shiree who waved a little in a parting, see you soon kind of way, and I said, "Is that all then Ralf?"

"That's it for now, thanks Randolph," he said as he directed me towards the door. I opened it and stepped once more into what already seemed a more familiar and comforting environment.

This building, this city, this life was demanding in ways I had in no way expected. Now I had real problems to think of. How would the real Randolph respond. I'm going to wait and see how I feel in a few days. It's not a crisis, it's normal, a little unusual but that's part of a human's life and the sooner I can get used to it the better.

12

I wanted to sort out my feelings for Miriam as soon as I could. When I got home that day I said I had met Rex and Ralf and everything had gone very well. I mentioned that Ralf had a new project for me and that we were going to talk about it while playing golf the next afternoon. She had to give me a quick run-down on what the game of golf entailed and I promised to give Ralf a good few holes as apparently I was used to doing, even though I thought it wasn't being honest.

"Well then we can go shopping in the morning," she said unexcitedly.

"What pray tell is shopping," said I, now feeling uninhibited about my ignorance.

"It's about time you made a study of the dictionary," said Miriam, "shopping is going to a building where goods are sold, things we need for the house; clothes, cleaning things, food and those sorts of things. You'll like it."

So the next morning we set out for a shopping centre where I was to see many earth products. Many of these products I would never have thought necessary and it must have taken all of recorded history to invent them all. Apparently necessity is not the prevailing principle.

At mid-morning Miriam and I stopped at a cafe for coffee and we had a good talk. "I have always encouraged you in your work Randy," she said in a consoling and soothing tone of voice. I could tell she was getting used to me being her Randy, her husband. "In this new project just do the best you can, you always surprise everyone but we know if you just do your best that's enough."

She gave me a big wide smile that seemed to melt all the snow on all the mountains of doubt that had been drifting in and out of my consciousness for the last week.

I was gradually becoming to appreciate Miriam as more than just a human being however I was not feeling the same male, female attraction as I had felt for Shiree. Time will tell.

13

Ralf and I met at the golf clubhouse at 2 o'clock. We made idle chit-chat for half an hour over a cup of coffee. He held an unlit cigar in his hand. "I used to be a heavy smoker, and then I switched to these. Now I just hold one occasionally. It's healthier than the fags." he smiled intimately. Then we strolled ever so slowly out onto the green. Ralf placed his ball onto the tee and swung high then low, "I can do that," I thought.

"Now this project," said Ralf slowly and quietly as though half the people on this planet were eager to know the details. "It's going to be big - a real tourist attractor - put us on the world map. And naturally I hope you won't forget me - remember the Putney Bridge - something that would give me some status to retire on, so to speak, get my drift?"

"Yes of course Ralf, I'll do the very best I can." I said.

"It's the West Park Fountain, it's getting old, it needs replacing, something spectacular, I had in mind a statue; really huge, and if it were to be named the Putney statue so much the better. I'll leave it to you. But I must admit that I will be eternally grateful for any favour you can do for Shiree and I so I'm willing to give you a free hand on this project. Yes Randolph, you do whatever pleases you; just think big."

He was so relaxed but I was listening to the birds as much as to him. If humans want to glorify themselves, well it's my job, I'll do my best.

We finished the eighteen holes in three hours with much silence, much peace of mind as I continued to watch and listen to the different kinds of birds that swooped and soared and hopped about the green carpet of the golf course.

It's a great game I was thinking but when we reached the last hole Ralf turned to me and said, "If you win this hole it will be the first time that you have beaten me," his bushy eyebrows were twitching. "I don't like to lose but I figure, what the heck, I'm going to be owing you so much soon what's one game of golf going to matter."

"Exactly," said I, "and I was only doing my best."

14

At breakfast the following morning I let Miriam know that I had beaten Ralf at my first game of golf. "But that's not like you," she said, "haven't I always said; oh you wouldn't remember; but I've told you to be nice to Ralf, he's your boss and even though I believe that you have much more talent at what you do than he ever thinks you capable of, it's just a game and I've said it hundreds of times. An ounce of discretion is worth a ton of honesty. You've always been too honest for your own good. Listen to me Randy next time let him win, he likes that, and he'll like you better."

"I'm sorry," I said "I forgot; I was watching the birds and I didn't realize my natural talent."

"That's just the trouble," she said earnestly, "you did realize your natural talent when sometimes, sometimes Randy, you have to think of others. You can't just let nature take it's course in golf or anything else."

"This new project is a big statue," I changed the subject, "And Ralf wants it to be some sort of glorification of himself like the Putney Bridge. But he said I could have a free hand this time; like if I wanted to do a Randolph Bilder statue wouldn't that be something."

"Yeh, I like that, you've earned it after what you have done for this city. I do like that .. the Randolph Bilder statue, a big statue of Randy; yes .. I like that a lot."

She was serious.

"I was only joking," I said. "I don't want to attract attention to myself; for Randolph's sake I might, but this is going to be a world tourist attraction, really big time, so I can't make out that I'm something special; if you know what I mean."

But Miriam liked the idea and so over the next few months she mentioned it almost every day.

"The Randolph Bilder Statue, world attraction; bigger than big; grander than grand," she would say these kinds of things, daydreaming.

She was thinking about me, Randolph, her husband. She wanted my life to be glorified, a testament not only to what I stood for as a husband, father, designer extraordinaire but as a human being. She did not seem to me to be gratifying herself as being the fortunate and no-doubt honourable wife of such a human. Her feelings were honestly for me, my edification, and I was flattered to believe that I, a normal, average human being could be valued so highly.

I thought deeply on this over the next few weeks even whilst feeling the desire quickening to have my way with Shiree; Shiree like a melody.

15

I tried to think about Shiree which wasn't hard to do and Ralf, and Shiree again but mostly I pondered this little dilemma that I felt warranted my preoccupation.

Miriam seemed totally unselfish and displayed such humility that I was wondering; is this only to do with the bond of marriage or could one show this spirit of humility for others. Could I Randolph Bilder put my ego aside and not think about myself or even Miriam, could I see what it would mean to Ralf and Shiree to have their own baby. Then my thoughts turned to Spin and Siri, the joy that they brought to Randolph and Miriam's lives. If I could bring myself; forget my own selfish and guarded scruples, to give of myself; I was sure I knew what to do.

Above all this, I reminded myself rationalizing like a person with a split-personality, trying to convince the real Randolph; I was an extra-terrestrial and I had an obligation to experience all that would normally occur in the life of an average human. I had a duty, yes that's it, a duty it was.

The way was clear as far as I was concerned, and as long as Miriam would never know, then I could see no problems. I felt a strong sense of relief at mastering this dilemma.

16

It was a few days later or sooner depending what was on my mind at any particular time. I had had impromptu meetings with Rex to discuss the new materials and processes, and possible combinations to produce an overall effect that as I said to him would, "blow their heads off." I found that I liked to encourage the staff's enthusiasm.

Although I had come to respect Rex's quick intelligence and astuteness I realized that being roughly ten years younger than myself he had great future potential and therefore I sought his opinion as regards to the significance of the project.

"Ralf wants to name the statue the Putney statue, does that inspire you?"

I was looking for some guide to how another staff member would view the ambitions of our manager.

"He already has the Putney Bridge, I think that should be enough for him. Sometimes he seems like a puffed-up egotist to me but he handles the staff so well that you might think he was dealing with the public. The Putney Bridge is a fantastic tribute to his work here but maybe it's time to give some credit where credit is due," said Rex.

Rex was enthused but I wondered what he meant. "What do you mean, Rex?" I said.

"Well," he smiled at me and replied, "Ralf is the driver of the Design Office but you are the engine."

17

It was five days since my return from holidays and since I had had that fateful meeting with Ralf. I was not surprised Friday morning when Rex said,

"Ralf wants to see you in his office."

"I suppose this is more guidelines for the West Park project," I said.

"Yes," said Rex "perhaps he wants a bust of himself."

"We'll see about that," I said intending to ask a little more from Ralf as it was within my power to do him the great favour that he was wanting.

I walked along the corridor with a sense of premonition. That room in the sky. My positive feeling. This could be interesting. I knocked and opened the door to Ralf's office. His secretary looked at me and at Ralf who was standing in his doorway gesturing me forward.

As I entered the skyroom Ralf waved me towards a large armchair where Shiree had sat, and he sat in another chair next to it.

"Well, let's get down to business. I want something from you and if I ever can return the favour you only have to ask." He paused, "So what's it going to be with you and Shiree." He spoke quietly.

"I have given it a lot of thought," I said, "and I can now assure you, Shiree's wish is my desire. I'm happy to agree."

"OK!" he said excitedly, his eye-brows twitching. "I'm arranging a; excuse the expression, naughty but nice, weekend for you and Shiree in Brookland. We'll mix business with pleasure. You are to meet the world famous sculptor Olivia Octavo there to discuss this West Park project. How does that sound to you?"

"The weekend sounds fine and I am especially pleased with the prospect of working with Olivia Octavo; how did you get her, one of her sketches alone would be worth millions." It was my turn to feel the excitement rise and I glanced out into the clouds to calm myself.

"At first she was a little reluctant but when I mentioned that she would be working with you she quickly agreed, she said, name your price. So there's a compliment for you. Also I was thinking this project could be a bust of me on a grand scale but the Landscape Architects office has been exceptional over the years so I'm going to give you more autonomy, you choose what it is to be , OK?" I could tell he was letting go of his dream reluctantly but he could hardly consider himself worthy of such an honour a second time. His immortal dreams would have to wait.

"Yes of course," said I "that's fine."

"Shiree will be in contact with you within the next two weeks. It's got to be very discreet though, you understand," again he was quietly spoken and self assured.

"Yes, discretion, Shiree, two weeks," I said, not quite believing that this good fortune had smiled upon me.

Ralf ushered me out of his skyroom; again I was glad to be in a more usual, comforting part of the Design Office building.

18

I worked solidly with Rex for a full two weeks with constructive and fruitful results. We found that the Uzbekistanis had been using moulds for pre-fab slabs of the boron\mercury crystals but I felt sure we could reduce the mix to a gas and spray it. But how could we give it shape, form.

Rex's research was very useful; he discovered the formula for directing the micro-lasers in definite patterns, ray patterns that could be programmed into any shape. Then we combined the two to produce a plan for directing the growth of the crystals by pre-determining the form of the micro-lasers. It was kind of moulding from within.

Now I had to seriously consider the subject for the sculpture. Some universal symbol I looked for, something producing a sense of wonder and instant identification. My job wasn't to be easy.

19

I had mentioned to Miriam that I would be going for a weekend to visit Olivia Octavo in Brookland. This seemed to be something that Randolph had done occasionally for researching this or that project. Randolph would be gone for a day or a weekend from time to time so this was not considered unusual.

It was one Monday morning when the drive to work had been particularly pleasant. I had been daydreaming whilst driving; Miriam, Shiree; Miriam, Shiree.

I was light-headed, filled with happiness and the fulfilling sense of anticipation.

Then as I was walking softly ever so softly to the wash-room Shiree came out of a side door. She was passing me before I could speak.

"Four o'clock at the coke machine," she whispered; soft, smooth, musically.

I sat for the next few hours looking out of my office window. I could see the traffic on a distant auto-way. I could see little people bustling towards who knew what destiny. I felt the metabolism of this city steadily intensifying as people were leaving their places of work to trek home or wherever people trek to; a drink after work, to meet someone, to browse the windows of the closing shops; perhaps to go to West Park to look at a future they had no idea would be.

Everything changes, is in flux, a universal flow.

Now I looked at the clock on my desk, it was almost four.

20

No one was at the coke-machine when I arrived. I waited; inserted a coin, the can tumbled, cold into my hand. Was I thirsty? I didn't know, but I held a secret longing in my soul. Soon I would be seeing her, soon I would be holding her, soon … Shiree sashayed casually up to the coke machine.

"We had to meet like this," she said in a restrained taut voice. "It's easy to arouse suspicion in this place and you know how people gossip." She slipped a coin into the slot and the can spun in the catcher trough. I downed a full half of my can; coke never tasted so good.

We seemed to stand looking into each others eyes for an eternity. I became aware of her tight fitting, low necked elegant dress and her gently rising and falling bosom.

I belched loudly as the coke bubbles burst tickling me inside, "Sorry," I said.

"That's OK," she smiled, she seemed to be looking deep into me, penetrating where no human had seen. Did she know?

"This envelope contains the plane ticket and details. We sit together on the plane." She paused and a distant music rushed ever louder into my awareness.

"Remember, we meet on the plane and no contact before. Is that clear, Randolph?" She was real, she wanted me; she wanted something from me that I had no memory of ever giving before.

"Yes, yes and thank you Shiree." I was in a trance, I forgot myself.

"Oh no, the thanks are all mine and Ralf's of course. So it's goodbye until later."

She stood back and gave me one long smiling look of appreciation.

"Goodbye Randolph." Music fading.

"Goodbye Shiree," I watched her move off down the corridor, her perfume lingering in the shimmering afterglow. She turned and gave me one last glance and entered a side door.

That's it! It's done! Well not quite. I stepped lightly back to my office. Just time to peruse the contents of the envelope before I go home to the family. That's it! No pangs of guilt, just the lingering of Shiree's scent about me and a slight shimmering in the air.

21

Time passes quickly and sometimes slowly reveals what one may have only an inkling of here in the ever present now. Moments group together, and hours hide daydreams that only seldom do we humans remember. I am starting to think like a real human being, I am starting to remember the passing fancies of a time before I, Randolph Bilder became Mr. Alien or Alien X as I preferred to refer to myself.

For days on end I look out my office window staring at this spectacle, this panorama of life. Or I would sit at my desk and all the while floods of abstract moodiness would sweep across my mind.

Once mountains appeared before my very eyes; hazy misty mountains. And there was a voice, monotonous ... "You learn these facts, theories, formulae; you who have a dream," and the voice formed a vista of mountains in my mind.

And then the voice trailed off, floating in the background of my mind. Now I could hear many muffled voices, the voices of young men and women, well almost men and women. I recognized faces; they are students, acquaintances of mine from university. The voices broke up into individual words and phrases linked together like the carriages of a train, a train that is winding, curving through a misty mountain range.

I hear the monotonous voice of a lecturer ... "You will make of these concepts, these ideas, a new world, a world more wonderful than we now dream of, for it is the material world where people are born and die, where civilizations rise and fall, and it will come to pass that what you now view as a mere process of learning is a very real and tangible dream; for it is" ... and here the voice trailed off again until it seemed but a memory. But a muffled chorus of voices repeated and continued ... "for it is the dreams that things are made of."

22

In my quiet evenings at home I found myself wanting to discover fragments of Randolph's past life; I found myself searching through drawers of belongings and old photo albums. Music was everywhere in my home; Siri practising the piano, Spin playing CD's, Miriam singing some song she had heard or was listening to on the radio. I was extremely comfortable here, like being in the womb of the world. I followed my feelings without thinking, turning pages of the albums, scanning photos of people, places - fragments from a past that I was increasingly getting a liking for.

On one such evening with a joyful feeling of mirth and shadowy reminiscing I came upon a large photograph of Miriam. It was an old photo; she was reclining naked with her arm outstretched towards the viewer. I didn't realize how long I had been staring into those eyes, following every curve of her body, caressing her long blonde hair and admiring the way her outstretched arm was reaching out, beckoning. I had as yet never seen anything so beautiful.

As I studied meticulously the curves, the flowing vibrant flesh I noticed that her belly was swollen. I realized that she must have been in the early stages of pregnancy. Was it Spin or was it Siri. I was going into a sublime hypnotic revelry and didn't stir until I felt a hand on my shoulder. Miriam was leaning over me, "Time for bed, sleepy head," that was all she said.

23

It was to be a three month wait until I flew out to Brookland. I was concentrating on the project. I worked constantly with Rex and when we felt that we had all the details I asked Rex to send the requirements for space, equipment and materials to the laboratory manager in the basement of the building. This was where we usually constructed scale models of our various projects.

Later that day the reply came. The tests could take place the following week, same day. Rex and I were now poised for the grand experiment. If our theories worked we would be ready to bring to the world something totally innovative, a real inspiration. As we were inspired so too could we inspire others.

24

There were certain things that I could not speak of to anyone, only Miriam. With Rex I let him do most of the calculations and tended to take a supervisory role; offering suggestions and giving him a major part in the design procedure. This may not have been how Randolph would have gone at it but I didn't trust myself, there were too many gaps in my knowledge of basic concepts. Then there was my complete inability to master the use of computers. The real Randolph would have found no problem with the various functions of computerization and the on the spot invention of new programming strategies.

I therefore felt a sense of relief to be able to speak freely with Miriam. The subject for the sculpture; that was the problem. I asked Miriam where I could find photographs of statues.

"In the library," she said, and to my puzzled look, "It's a large building where books are kept."

25

Miriam gave me directions to the main public library. The next morning I travelled into the city but I didn't go to the Design Office, instead I went to a library. It was my first time wandering down isles of books that were on shelves rising up above my head. I found the area where the sculpture books were kept and began a day long search. I saw all manner of sculpting styles, all kinds of materials from everywhere on the planet. I was mainly interested in contemporary sculpture although I found large figures representing the Buddha rather fascinating.

It was later in the day when I found a book simply titled:

JERRY DUNKWORTH
SCULPTURE

The pictures inside at first appeared to be huge boulders with tiny people standing in the foreground. At closer examination I could see that the boulders were figures, reclining, sitting and suggesting a primordial unconscious imagery. I was thoroughly taken with this sculptor. I asked the woman at the counter if I could get copies of the photos. She looked at the front of the book and said that the artist had given permission for these photos to be reproduced. I asked her if she could do it for me, and she took me to a machine not far away and photocopied twenty pages of the book. I took the photograph of Miriam out of my pocket; I had been carrying it just to look at, and asked her if she could copy that as well. She did and then, looking at the photo, said that it was very beautiful. She identified with it very appreciatively. That done, I was ready for Brookland and Olivia Octavo.

26

First things first, that seemed to be a Randyism. Rex and myself had to run the tests on the materials and processes. We walked together to the lift and were shortly in the basement. I was introduced to the laboratory manager.

"Hi, Randolph, long time no see. I'm glad you have something for me, and how's Miriam?" I was taken aback, I could remember the face but his name escaped me. We were like a large family or tribe in the Design Office. Everyone knew everyone else more or less as I was realizing each passing day.

"Good morning sport," said I, "and Miriam is fine thanks."

Well everything was set up. We had the correct amount of boron and the right weight of mercury. The oxidizer and centrifugal pump were in place, the space was neatly set out. So we started; we had decided that a small cube would be the ideal shape of the test model. Rex switched on all the machines and set the oxidizer going. Then he sat with a lap-top to record the process.

At first nothing happened but then gradually from the base of the bench a square shape formed. I adjusted the Bunsen burners to get a slower build up. Slowly the shape was forming; a white shape definitely becoming that of a cube. Several hours later we turned off the oxidizer and centrifugal pump.

There was a cube, white like ice-cream and it had a shimmering glow about it. It was plugged into the energy source to keep the micro-lasers operating. One flick of a switch and we supposed the cube would disappear. It was magnificent; we stood in awe gazing at the shimmering cube.

"If only we could add colour to it," I said, "if we could filter the micro-laser beams through a prism we might have a colour field effect."

"What colour would you want?" said Rex.

"Let's try for a rainbow," I said, wanting to replicate that awesome natural phenomenon.

The next step which seemed quite comical was to test the cube's water resistance. The Lab manager stood over the cube with an ordinary garden watering can. He poured and the water splashed in streams down over the cube and down the sides of the cube. We now knew that our invention was weatherproof.

27

Later that same day I found myself standing. I seemed taller than usual, looking out of my window. A sudden pang of triumph gripped my consciousness and radiated throughout my body. I was ecstatic to think that I Randolph Bilder; master of the material world, creator of things past and things yet to be, had achieved what could become one of the greatest wonders of all time.

I felt a stirring in the genital area as though a small bird with little ruffled feathers was stirring in it's nest. The tiny bird lurched into the crisp air, crisp with omnipotence and plunged, soaring, upwards on ever rising spirals the cool halcyon air stream. I knew I had experienced this feeling of exhilaration before, when I had built the Putney Bridge, the Chrome Crab and the Space Observatory but this time would be my crowning achievement, the ultimate gift of Alien X.

The day before I was to depart to Brookland and Olivia with the delectable Shiree I strutted proudly into the Landscape Architects office. Rex was there to greet me.

"Martin has something to report on the cube," he said.

"Martin, who's Martin?" I said.

"The Lab Manager, I thought you knew him," Rex replied.

"I don't see him that often but I remembered his face," I said apologetically.

I walked into the lab excitedly to see my great creation once again. There it was glittering, shining; a perfect cube. This time however it was multi-coloured with rainbow hues and had a fine shimmering aura. I didn't notice Martin standing nearby.

"It's magnificent!" he seemed as excited as I was.

We stared some moments at the stark spectacle of light. Then he said stammering, "It's amazing, and the thing is that as time passes it becomes much denser, much stronger. It's already harder than any known material on earth; surely it must reach an optimum density, a cut off point where it cannot possibly get any denser."

"Just reduce the energy quotient," I said, "until it requires no additional supply of extraneous input of any kind." I wanted to see it be self sufficient; an entity existing concretely, eternally.

"The crystals grew according to the programmed specifications and then it just got denser and harder. It's amazing!" he was awestruck.

"Well, we will see what happens on a larger scale in a couple of months." I was trying to remain calm, "I'm going to Brookland tomorrow, wish me luck."

That night I couldn't sleep. Although I had found sleep a fascinating state of consciousness to be in. To lose oneself every night; to charge the batteries, I had thought, but I didn't dream. Being awake was like a dream to me or what I fancied a dream might be like. I saw shapes and colours just before I lost consciousness each night and then again when I awoke each morning. But this night I couldn't sleep. I tried to lie still hoping the calm body state would produce a corresponding state of mind.

I couldn't help thinking of Randolph's parents. Miriam had told me that they lived in a place called Snug Falls where my father still worked as a part time tour guide. It was a kind of nature park where people from the city could see unusual animals; it was where Randolph had spent his childhood.

Perhaps Randolph had some unconscious longing to see his parents. I as Alien X, had put off visiting them. Surely they would know that there was something strange about me, perhaps distant and more formal than they had known me to be. Maybe the real Randolph had a desire to see them again. I don't know, but it kept me awake most of the night, trying to imagine Randolph's parents into being, to see their faces and I also wondered what Snug Falls would be like.

I felt less than refreshed when after only about an hour's sleep Miriam turned towards me.

"Good morning .. are you ready for your first flight?"

"As ready as I'll ever be," I said, shaking rainbow colours out of my awareness.

The morning was fine, hot and hazy; one of those first days of summer when you have a premonition of all the hot days that await there in that long summer season. I would have felt this way had I been the real Randolph but as it was I just felt a sense of justness and rightness in the world as I looked out of the lounge room window.

Miriam and the children were scurrying about, washing up after breakfast. They were coming with me to the airport, the kids love to see the planes she said. As we walked out the door I said, just a moment, and popped into Spin's bedroom where I slipped one of his CD's into my briefcase. Then off along the auto way, Miriam drove.

The children were quiet with anticipation. When we arrived at the airport the children became very excited. Siri was jumping about and Spin pointed at everything that moved. I was soon walking into the boarding tunnel and waving over my shoulder to Miriam and Spin and Siri who waved back frantically. Then I entered the jet.

31

Seat 7; 8; 9, and there she was demure, cute and smaller looking in her big plane seat. I sat next to her as she was sitting next to the window. She was smiling wide and welcoming.

"Shiree, good day" I exclaimed.

"And good day to you, so good to see you," she purred.

It went like this, chatty at first and then becoming more serious as we were very aware of what was in store for us. I asked what perfume she was wearing, she said opium. Apparently it had been a favourite essence since her childhood in Hong Kong. Her mother was a native of Hong Kong and had immigrated down here with her husband, a British public relations executive and Shiree. Shiree had been fourteen then. She still spoke a little Mandarin. Actually she was a linguist. When I asked about her work she said that it was mainly for the media and was connected with associates in Hong Kong.

We spoke easily, breezily. And when I asked to look out the window she kissed my cheek as I leaned over, that's for later, she said. Then I changed places with her to get a better view of that spectacular sky, clouds and the tiny rivers and towns on the ground. I was again feeling a sense of exhilaration, thoughtless, like every second mattered so very much.

We went from the airport by taxi to a hotel in central Brookland it had on the front, The Mirador Hotel and it was very tall. We had eaten on the plane even though we had only been in the air for two hours. Being unusually hungry we went into the cafeteria of the hotel for some light snacks. It was extremely pleasant and I was surprised when Diana Kraul's voice and piano sang out; piped music for pleasure. I felt contented and a wave of peacefulness and tiredness swept over my body.

32

Shiree was extremely exciting, intoxicating to the point of weariness. I was very tired. She noticed and said could we take a siesta. Spanish custom she explained, she didn't plan to waste any time apparently.

So we went up to our room, all the way up. It was a penthouse suite with enough space to accommodate a large family easily.

I hadn't brought pyjamas as the weather was so hot. "Skip the formalities, let's go to bed, at least we will remember each others body smells," she rolled the words out like she was eager, but oh, so confident.

As I plumped down on the grand sized bed the softness of the linen rose around me like a thin cloud. I closed my eyes and started to see colours and the primordial figures of Jerry Dunkworth shadowy, wavering in the filtered light.

Next she was upon me, her naked taut flesh rolling over me like a slippery snake, she must have put some sort of oil over her body. I was quickly as oily as she and moving in sync with her thrashing, twisting form that writhed upon my quivering body. Steam seemed to rise from our combined flesh as I entered her or rather as she lowered herself down on me. We were tangled in a living dream that as I drifted away on floods of pure pleasure took me deeper into a cave of dark warmth and contentment.

33

"We did it," I said dreamily as I awoke early the next morning and went straight back to sleep. We slept long and late. A stream of light beamed happily across the shady room from the slightly parted curtains.

"We did it last night. Like the first time for me, Alien X, about to beget a space-age baby. But was it like that with Miriam. That was what we did to make Spin and Siri and so many times before and after. Was it the same, not the same, no."

"Not quite the same," I was repeating to myself as Shiree moved like a dozing kitten.

34

It was mid-day before I got off in a taxi to Olivia's mansion on the outer limits of Brookland. As we drove up to the gates I was surprised to see large gates with many grotesque, gothic looking faces peering out; adorning the gate, which opened when the taxi driver spoke into a hand phone on the pillar of the gate.

The taxi left me in front of a sweep of steps leading up to a three story Georgian house covered in ivy. The drive way had been sided by a tall hedge so I was as yet to see Olivia's garden, the garden of delights.

35

Olivia greeted me warmly and familiarly.

"I live here alone with my servants," she said, "I am very rich. You can't bribe me," she laughed. "I do exactly as I please and I never compromise. My only criterion is beauty, of course my criterion is not always the same as my critics but then I am an established artist so people know what to expect."

"However I would be pleased to work with such a talent as yourself. I've heard very many good things about you, your work I mean. Yes," she mused "and I've seen, actually seen with my own eyes that Chrome Crab, that huge crab. What an imagination you must have," she paused.

"Of course Ralf Putney has been in touch with me recently and he has said that you have come up with something really exciting, some new material or process. I can't wait to hear about it."

So I explained the new invention and she was very impressed, she actually licked her lips; possibly picturing in her mind how the combination of her skills and experience could fit in with this new approach to sculpture. "It's sort of sculpting from within," I said.

Next thing, everything going smoothly and very accommodatingly I thought; we were stepping down the sweep of the front entrance of the house to a side gate, again with grotesque faces leering and laughing, seemingly at me.

The garden was not what I was expecting. I had pictured a well manicured, lawned and hedged design perhaps with a fountain or two. What greeted me was a jungle first of low bushes and climbing plants tumbling one over the other. Then there were larger trees and further away very large trees sprawling and wild looking.

She seemed to find a path where I could see none and she led me passed a number of large statues. These statues were of fairies, witches and wizards, all in the same grotesque style as the faces on the gates. This time it was complete bodies, posturing; leaning and gesturing in a strange and mysterious way towards me. I felt strongly affected by these figures and the wild nature of her overgrown garden.

Each statue was of several figures and behind them, part of each statue, was a cliff face or waterfall of glistening stone. She explained that these were all designed to be placed against walls. All these sculptures were non-commissioned favourites but, she said confidentially, they were all for sale at a price.

As we continued to wander I felt swallowed up in this world of grotesque mystery. For a while, lost; and yet found, in my consciousness yielding to this fantastic world of delights.

36

As we were walking up the steps at the entrance of her house I glanced sideways at this curious person. She had a serious thin smile and I felt very affected by her as well as her creations. Impressed is the word but perhaps she had this effect on everyone and not just me.

"I'm very impressed by your works," she said as if she could read my mind. We entered a large courtyard somewhere within the house.

"Just what did you have in mind as a possible subject for this commissioned sculpture of mine?" she continued.

"I have these photographs of some works by a sculptor named Jerry Dunkworth. Do you know of him? I replied.

"Jerry Dunkworth! Why of course, who do you think I am, an alien! Everyone on my planet has heard of Jerry," she declared.

I of course was shocked. Another alien I thought. The implication was to close for comfort.

"And I've even met him," she went on. "He's in the same area as myself, large outdoor pieces but I don't think that I could work in his style. By the way he's a quietist; did you know? He never speaks to anyone." She seemed thoroughly amused at my suggestion of Jerry.

"I had hopes … but … anyway, take a look at these photos, could you?" I was quite disappointed, though still mystified by this strange person, Olivia.

"Yes; well," she said after looking at most of the photographs," very kind of subliminal and rather primitive, not quite what I'm about. But wait, this is nice; yes this is very beautiful. Is it Jerry's work?"

I looked inquisitively at the photo in her hand, "No! That's a photo of my wife!" said I, rather surprised.

"I could do that," she said, "Yes I would like to do this!"

"Well I believe it's a beautiful rendition of her, however, I don't know. Give me some time," I said, thoughts escaping me. "I hadn't expected, but, if you truly like it … "

"Like it, I love it; it's very classical. Not what I usually do, but it's so, so beautiful." Her enthusiasm was spontaneous and contagious. But on she went, "The reclining pose, the outstretched arm, and isn't she a little pregnant? She would be so lovely filled with rainbows."

That was it, I found myself wanting it too, convinced, "I'll speak to my assistant Rex Gonzales who receives equal credit for the new materials invention. He and I will formulate some co-ordinates for density and get the proportions and dimensions in order. Is it OK to have an extra month to complete the data?"

"Well yes that's fine, don't change your mind meanwhile, promise?"

"I promise Olivia."

37

On my way back to the Mirador Hotel I decided to walk a few blocks of this large city, to experience a new environment. A human life is full of unexpected lessons, I reasoned, what would I learn this day in this bigger than big city of Brookland. I did not wish to miss out on what promised to be a valuable lesson oh no; as I was coming to realize the human heart has a large capacity for curiosity.

As I strolled along the streets of Brookland this hot summer evening I found a vibrant, populous distraction. But was it to be only this, no!

Here I saw a young woman walking, so fresh so cute I, I wanted to kiss her. And there, more young women; long hair short hair, curly hair straight hair, slim with tight fitted pants and short skirts; with colours and patterns of every variety. They seemed to present themselves deliciously for my eyes only. My head was swirling; so this is love, I thought, that emotion I had heard sung of. I remembered the words of a song; "Love is a thing of wonder, love and never let it go." Well, this was love at a distance.

These women were not aware of my feelings. They sped with purposes unknown, their hearts and minds with some secret desire to reach each a destination not known to me. They were unaware of this feeling of love that swelled uncontrollably and spread in warm vibrations all over me.

Love can exist apart from love's object then, I reasoned. Could love exist apart from my feelings. Could I be some one's love object and not even know. In fact could this feeling of love which had formed into an idea in my mind, could it exist independent of both subject and object. The very idea of love, floating above us. In other words, was it an omnipresent and perhaps universal spiritual value or essence? I found myself gripped by a private desire to return to my home planet to see for myself if love existed there.

So lessons produced more questions than answers, I thought. But if I could protect these people from earthly danger, if I could make their futures bright then I would, Yes I whispered aloud, as I entered the Mirador Hotel, "I will, I will!"

But then, safe within the grandiose spaces of the Mirador lobby I thought, "Maybe they don't need an alien protector."

38

"What's your favourite book," said Shiree inquisitively.

"The dictionary," I said as I mixed a coke at the apartment's lounge bar.

"Oh, how interesting but not surprising for an engineer or architect; whatever you may be; professionals like you aren't often as cultured as some people."

"I have a secret desire to communicate better, and the dictionary I find can be a great friend," I was being coolly intellectual like I guess, the real Randolph.

"Yes well, being a linguist I have an almost natural love for words; words like, succedaneum and hagiocracy."

"My curiosity is aroused," I coolly replied.

"Succedaneum - substitute or a drug that can be prescribed in place of another. I figure that I am in some way a succedaneum; a substitute for Miriam. But I am like a passing whim, you'll perhaps forget me in a couple of months, anyway we hope something good will come of it."

"Yes, something good will come of it." I was tending to be a little guarded with Shiree. Normally humans take many risks but I, an alien could not allow risk taking, perhaps only with Miriam. Shiree could never be a .. succedaneum, for Miriam.

"And the other one, what was it? Words don't naturally have a lasting meaning for me unless they have concrete benefits. Do you think I'm too self concerned?"

"No not at all, I believe that's quite normal. You wouldn't be human if you weren't a little selfish," she quipped. I wondered.

"The other one was hagiocracy .. a state or community governed by holy people." She stated her fact.

"Holy, you mean religious?" I was puzzled.

"More or less, it's like there are several thousand; I call them shining lights; people who are showing the way, guiding humanity, on this planet. It's a hagiocracy on this earth. And I figure you are one of these shining lights, a real inspiration." Shiree was serious and looked at me with great respect, I thought.

"Oh you truly believe that, why?" I asked.

"All these new designs, new ways of building, they're providing solutions to the worlds problems; it's not the same with Ralf, he seems to feel that, it's not what you do but the way you do it. He's great with people but he doesn't change things, not really."

Her honesty caused me to put more trust in her, more faith perhaps; but I was still puzzled.

"But Ralf has a very responsible position. He can do so many things that I couldn't even dream of," I continued interestedly.

"Yes and you've got to admire him. When I first met him he had just started at the Design Office, in the public relations department. My father was a public relations executive like Ralf and they were friends and business associates. Ralf's father had worked for an engineering company, a machinist, but he wanted the best for Ralf. So Ralf worked his way through Uni and got a job here at the Design Office. He's got where he is today through sheer hard work. He's a whiz with people but he really doesn't match what you do."

"Well, I have a talented associate to work with, Rex Gonzales, my assistant; I couldn't do what I do without being part of a team. Actually I owe a lot to Rex." I said trying to explain my true feelings.

"Well perhaps he'll be a shining light too, God knows we need all we can get."

It was a wonder to me how Shiree could make so much of mere words, play around with them. She seemed to paint mountains where there was only a page in a dictionary, with only words on it; well, and meanings, and what words meant was so important. The search for meaning; to see clearly out of the swirling pool of our emotions, that, I felt must be the greatest challenge for the average human. It seems easy to co-ordinate and control our bodies but how does the mind control itself? Questions, always more questions.

39

It was later in the evening after a truly wonderful dinner in the dining room of the Mirador Hotel.

"Want to hear something besides piped music?" I said, curious myself.

"Yes, why not?" Shiree replied playfully.

"This is it," I said, "my son's CD."

Shiree looked at the CD cover, intrigued. "The Attack of the Fungoidios," she read acceptingly, "so that's what he's into."

"Don't know myself but let's give it a go." I found myself coming up with complete Randyisms; they must be. I slipped it gently into the lounge CD player, it's mouth seemingly hungry since we returned from dinner.

A rippling sound, kind of whirring began to affect itself on the surround sound system of the penthouse suite. Then a rhythmic, randomly thumping, wafting in the corners of the lounge room like muffled footsteps. The creaking of a door on worn hinges sounded somewhere near the terrace and a soft, mellow tone droned ever louder in rising and falling waves.

"Sounds like moody stuff," said Shiree, "and what mood are you in?" She stood.

I couldn't help at that point but be aware how youthful she was. She was shorter without high heels, I noted. She loped over to the bar. The music was having a disorienting effect on me and I was becoming very self- conscious; or aware that we were alone, and that we were here for a purpose.

After pouring herself a long drink she took a long gulp and came nearer to where I was standing, as I obviously observed her every movement. She wasn't shy, she brushed her lips closer to my face, I could feel them. Then she kissed me with flicked tongue into my mouth, in and out rhythmically, in time with the pulsating sounds. One hand came around my neck and pressed my head closer, the other brushed below my waist. She fumbled with my fly zip. My penis thrust forward needing little provocation.

As I held her she rubbed her body against mine. Then drawing apart from me she said, "Let's get to bed," in a teasing little girl voice, so cute. Putting her hand in mine she purred, "Love me hard and love me deep."

"Oh yes! I will Shiree, I will," I gasped as I followed her into the bedroom.

40

I caught the early morning flight while Shiree stayed on in Brookland an extra day; shopping time, she had said. I felt exhilarated, tired and filled with a new sense of having achieved my first sexual encounter as a human being. Although it had been difficult to say goodbye to Shiree I looked forward to seeing Miriam who was to meet me at the airport.

As I walked calmly out of the arrivals tunnel I could see Miriam near the gates. She smiled and waved as if I had just returned from another planet. I was eager to tell her about my successful meeting with Olivia and feeling not at all as though I would have to hide my adventures with Shiree, my naughty but nice weekend.

Miriam flooded into my arms and we kissed more passionately than I can ever remember. She was a more heavily built woman than Shiree and I was aware of a yielding softness and pleasant odour, the odour of familiarity. Those eyes, I thought, they hold a tenderness that promises great things. If only I can prove my love or Randolph's love to her as it was before. I felt sure I could do this and then love would reign in our relationship.

I drove home and was aware that my city seemed somehow changed as though the heat haze of Brookland had settled over it.

41

Several days passed without event. I returned to work and informed Ralf of the progress made on two fronts. Then one evening at home I heard Spin playing *that* CD as I stepped near to his room. I began to think how Spin had gotten that funny name, Sojosafao. I asked Miriam of the origins of the name when we were alone.

We were married only a year, and we went for a holiday to Northern Rivers Adventure Resort. We had gone white water rafting, the boat had tipped over and Miriam had nearly drowned. She had been rescued by a native boy, a boy who had been adopted by a Portuguese family. They had named him Sojosafao and so when we had our first baby we named it after the boy who had saved her life. And so it is, another mystery solved.

42

During the next month and more Miriam and I became more intimate. We were now not afraid to touch each other, to hug each other spontaneously, and to kiss. I remember her kisses, slow, moist, soft and sweet; oh so sweet were her kisses.

The morning after one night of love making she said, "and what where you thinking of when we made love."

I said I felt the passion flowing through my gills. I had been a fish in her ocean of love.

"Very strong image," she said, "are you sure you weren't an alien fish where you came from?"

"That I may never know," I said philosophically.

Then later I said, "Will you get pregnant again?"

"No I've been taking contraceptive pills over the years to stop me having babies," she replied. "We only wanted two children. I would however be curious to see what a space baby would be like."

"That we may never know," I continued not to be speculative even though I knew there would be one space baby on this planet, Shiree's child, the space age baby.

43

I worked with Rex and he worked with the computer. He checked co-ordinates of proportion and thoroughly explored every area of dimension. We wanted a huge statue that would surprise everyone.

I spent whole days doing clueless crosswords and logic problems that I had usually left to Miriam. She liked to do these but I found them very difficult. Also I read the encyclopaedia although there were too many extraneous facts, too much information that I would have no earthly use for. My main occupation however was studying the dictionary. I read the largest dictionary I could find from cover to cover and many meanings I found I could remember in the months that followed.

Approximately one month after my meeting with Olivia Rex said he was as ready as he would ever be so we contacted Olivia. She wanted more and more information and complete details.

One thing bothered her however, a thing called the afferent nature of the growth of the crystals. She was puzzled and felt that we needed to define the ability of the micro-lasers to force the crystals as they grew into specific centres. This was one of the principles with which she always worked.

Rex was also puzzled at this request and together by linking computers and after another month's daily conferring they found a solution.

Olivia was now satisfied that we could go ahead and Rex was pleased to be done with this most arduous task. We were ready to begin.

44

I felt free now to indulge every whim of my imagination whilst sitting in my office or staring down out of the office window. I found myself day- dreaming of what I hoped would be my next project, the building of an aquarium, a huge aqua world.

Then I imagined the time I could plan ahead until the completion of the West Park statue. I saw people like islands; Ralf, Olivia, Rex rising out of a glistening sea and I like the captain of a ship steering carefully between them into a harbour, my destination, my goal.

45

The site at West Park was being cleared and I could see no problem until the actual construction began. Then it would be only a matter of letting the equipment function, the process to evolve and the statue of Miriam to rise, beckoning, as the sky grew a little closer.

It was Monday morning when totally unexpected Rex came into my office.

"I'm resigning," he said, "I've decided I can do more good in this world apart from the City Design Department. I'm taking our invention to the third world, and I'm going to build housing that lasts forever."

"I'm shocked," said I, "I never knew you cared so much. I thought your work here with me meant everything to you. If you feel that what you want to do cannot be left to others then it's your choice, but remember the Design Centre has a long history of promotion from within, not bringing in new talent but nurturing our own. You could have a fine future here, just consider that." I was reacting as I thought a superior should but in my heart I felt that I couldn't find another assistant like Rex. He had been with us about twelve years, I had read his department file, he had a family too, and I was confused to think that I would have to go on alone in the Landscape Architects Office. It would not be easy to find a replacement for Rex.

46

In the staff cafeteria that afternoon I picked up a local newspaper to help pass a few moments and not think too much about Rex's resignation. There on the front page the headline stared back at me.

CLASSIC STATUE: REVOLUTIONARY DESIGN

The article went on to say, and mention the names of Rex and I, Olivia Octavo, as well as Ralf Putney; as being new age geniuses, leading lights of architectural design and a great credit to the City. Spectators were welcome to witness the construction of the statue which it said promised to be a revelation in the processes of building. The statue would be completed within three months, the article finished.

Of course similar things had been said about the Putney Bridge, the Chrome Crab and the Observatory but this time, the statue being of my own wife, I felt a personal victory.

As I was walking towards the doors several staff members stopped to congratulate me, the sense of pride was a great reward in itself.

47

Rex was gone within the month of waiting for the construction to begin. We were sure that Martin from the laboratory and I could manage and direct the actual construction process once the equipment was in place.

Martin and I were present every day once the construction began. We had to supervise the supply of feeder material and keep the equipment in functioning order. We also had to monitor every step and supervise the foremen on the site. From the start the excitement of a large crowd of spectators and journalists kept us in a very alert and aware state. We followed the measurements and adjusted the dials of many machines, as to a large extent Rex had stipulated.

It was slow, this crystal formation. It took days before the barest hint of a shadow appeared on the large concrete base. Then as each day passed a little more of the figure took shape. Gradually the figure appeared to rise, shimmering as it formed and slowly the legs became visible; then the buttocks and then up to the waist. The tops of the legs formed like a mermaid appearing from the sea, and then the chest and back, and slowly the shoulders.

It was a triumphant day when the outstretched arm took shape and gesturing, beckoning; just as in the photograph which I held up in my field of view, with the almost complete statue behind.

As the head and face formed people began to cheer for it must have seemed as if they were witnessing a miracle. No-one as yet recognized the identity of the figure and as the machines were switched off and the energy supply gradually reduced I saw the aura of deflected micro-lasers put a final mystic touch to the statue.

There it was, in all it's glory, with rainbow colours transecting every inner space of it, seemingly emphasizing the muscular tone and giving it a reality which transcended anything that anyone had yet seen.

It's classic form and the pregnant state of the figure added a mystical permanence to what seemed to be a vision that could not be lastingly real. Such beauty was meant for transient things and evoked a sense of awesome luxury. I was overcome and tears trekked down my cheeks, "I know," said Martin as he handed me a packet of tissues, and then a murmur went up from the crowd. There had been a hush on first sight of the complete statue but now there was talk and merriment.

"This will have ever-lasting meaning for the whole world," declared Martin.

48

"Why!" said Miriam the next day when I took her to see the statue, "it looks exactly like me, except for the rainbows and the huge size. The pose, the face; exactly like that photo we had done when I was pregnant with Spin .. tell me, is it me?"

"Yes." I said, "and take a look at the inscription on this plaque."

Miriam lent forward and read:

MIRIAM BILDER
A WONDERFUL WIFE, A LOVING MOTHER AND A BEAUTIFUL HUMAN BEING

Miriam was quiet and then she cried, profusely. "It's too, too much," she sighed

49

"Family values, wonderful Randolph," said Ralf at a meeting in his office the day after I presented Miriam with the effigy of my love, the statue.

"You would be a whiz at public relations. That inscription kind of tugs at the heart strings of this city and therefore I have no hesitation in recommending to the board that you take my place at the end of the financial year. What do you say?"

"It would be an honour Mr. Putney," I said.

"Oh no! Please call me Ralf, how many times do I have to tell you?"

"However I have to decline for it would be far too difficult to come up with a replacement for Rex Gonzales and he, I assume, would have been the one to take my place as head of Landscape Architecture. As it is we will find it almost impossible to replace him." I was sure of what I was saying, Rex was invaluable, "If only we could entice him back in some way, isn't there anything that you can do?"

"I'll try," he said "I .. I'll do what I can." He was very accommodating. I felt he would do anything to have me as Manager of the Design Office and I felt also admiration for him just because he was willing to try so hard, always trying to please; the staff, the public and he did care so very much for Shiree.

50

A week later was the big day, the opening ceremony for the statue. It was too large to unveil but an elaborate protocol was in order that day. The Mayor gave a speech to television cameras and thousands of spectators. Ralf gave his speech which was rather short; I felt that he was another one who would not under any circumstances take risks, especially when dealing with the media. Olivia Octavo was also in attendance, and what a fine sight she was too, as she received a bouquet of flowers.

I was presented with a large water colour painting of the statue, with gold frame and the inscription for the statue printed below it. There was a lot of kissing and hugging and shaking hands then, to my surprise an older couple stepped up onto the stage. I recognized them immediately from old photos I had seen; they were my parents. I couldn't help it, tears came to my eyes as I embraced them both and then individually. This really was an exciting heart warmer for them and myself. It was to be one of my best days on planet earth.

51

I was sitting on the veranda of our house in the suburbs. The night was hot, I was drifting in my thoughts of the past few months; so this was the life of an average human, it was very exciting.

I was watching the stars in the clear night sky. They were very beautiful, very evocative of the great universe of which no-one seemed to know the actual dimensions. I was absent-mindedly searching this great expanse of stars presented before me like a great feast, when I became aware that one star was yellow in colour and seemed to be pulsating. I stared at this star for some time and found myself entranced, oblivious of any other sight or sound.

It was then that I felt a beam of vibrations hit my staring eyes and this beam seemed to telescope my consciousness transforming it into a receiver of a now, familiar sound and feeling.

I could hear water and the sudden bursting of small bubbles in some ocean deep. The rhythm of the bursting bubbles seemed to communicate a message to me. I concentrated to be more aware and soon knew what the message was.

Then the sounds ceased and I became aware of looking at a star again, an ordinary star; the same as millions of others, just twinkling there, there in the darkened night sky.

52

Before going to bed that same night I was eager although saddened to have to inform Miriam that I had received my message, I had been called home to my own planet. I would have to leave earth, leave Miriam and Spin and Siri; and all of my friends. It was a sad thing to say but at the same time I felt a private longing to be gone, to be home and with my own creatures, whatever they may be.

Miriam was saddened too and even surprised.

"I had gotten used to you," she said, "and I believed that you would be with me for years, perhaps forever." She paused considering perhaps how it would now have to be with her old Randy back in her world; the old humour that she said she had missed at first. She was accustomed to my stiff, formal, matter of fact existence and now I would be gone, gone from her earthly world of delights and challenges.

53

"Well Randolph," said Ralf jovially, "you will have to wait for your full promotion. The board has approved a new plan." This was at a meeting called in Ralf's office, the sky room.

"Yes Randolph, the board has chosen to keep me on as a part-time adviser and you will spend half your time as Manager of the Design Office and the other half training a new recruit to the Landscape Architects Department. We have hired a live wire; young, smart and one of the best of his generation. But don't feel that you will have to do it alone, we have someone to help you as part-time supervisor.

To my surprise Rex walked into the room, apparently awaiting his cue. He smiled amiably and shook my hand.

"Good day Randolph! Nice to be back on the team," he said.

"The board," Ralf continued, "has decided to sponsor Rex's third world housing projects so he will work with you and the new trainee part-time, and instruct building contractors from many poor countries too. It looks like it's going to work out very well; yes, very well don't you think Randolph?"

"Oh yes," I said very pleased to have a mutual solution to our problems. "I merely celebrate the power of dreams it is for younger awakened people like Rex to bring that power to fruition, out there in the real world."

I gazed at each of them and then light-headedly out of the windows at the amazingly displayed collection of clouds that Ralf keeps hidden from unsuspecting eyes in his office - his sky office which I, as Alien X would never occupy and neither the position of Manager of the Design Department, that would be left for Randolph Bilder when he awakens one morning.

54

"Mmmmmm, good morning Randy," said Miriam drowsily.

"What! Oh yes ... good morning Miriam," replied Randy Bilder.

"and how are you this morning," queried Miriam as she sat up in bed.

"Guess what! Miriam, I have had the strangest dream. In my dream I went to a planet in outer space. I occupied the body of a space person. I lived with the fish people who had arms and legs, and were amphibious," Randy strained to say it all at once.

"Yes, Randy! And then what happened?" Miriam stared at her husband and smiled.

PART 2

Alien X and the Second Visitation

My second visit to planet Earth was deemed necessary by the inhabitants of my home planet. They had long term and extensive plans of which I was as yet unaware. By the end of my second visit I could tell what those plans were. I shall inform the reader of my adventures, the challenges and the thrills of which there were many and various.

As I once more accustom myself to inhabiting an earthly body I find myself more relaxed and certain that as each day passes I shall reward my human host, Randolph Bilder, and his wife, Miriam Bilder; also my plans now reach out to humanity in an effort to join two worlds - two worlds although they be planets in distant reaches of the universe - worlds of people nonetheless capable of living in harmony, in close proximity.

ALIEN X
Spring 2029

55

Miriam Bilder awoke with a sense of premonition. Her husband Randy had worked very hard for many years on a personal project for which he claimed work time from the City Design Office where he was the manager. Recently he had said that his research was almost complete and he was ready for something to happen in his life, something for which he had lived and breathed for five long years.

"Good morning Randy, and how are you this morning," Miriam stretched, yawned and sat up in their bed.

"Good morning Miriam, well yes I am feeling fine; yes exceptionally fine this time." Randolph sat up alert and blinking into the bright morning light from the windows.

"Oh!" said Miriam, "what do you mean *this time.*"

"Well Miriam, just take it easy now and remember how some time ago you were visited by an alien ... well I'm back again," said Randolph.

"Oh! It's you again. You know I had a feeling something was bothering Randy, and

now I know,

"Yes, now we know. Randy has gone back to where you come from and you ... you

are here."

There was a long stretch of quietness as they looked about them, sometimes glancing at each other and adjusting to the new situation.

"Randy told me a lot about the planet you come from, the planet of the fish people. Do you remember your home planet?" said Miriam curiously.

"No," said Randolph, "I will have no memory of my past but I remember you well Miriam and I have had strange longings to be with you again. But that's not why I returned to Earth it is because my work is not finished. In fact it may never be finished however I will be going home some day soon and I will tell you when I'm leaving."

"Oh Randy, I don't mind that it's you; I have been happy with my husband and he has been a delight from one day to the next, year after year, but we thought this time would come when he could do no more on the work you both seem to be involved in."

"Well I have no idea what work we are concerned about and I am surprised to learn that I come from some fishy ancestors on a planet of fish people. Some time you can tell me more about them but now I want to have breakfast with Spin and Siri, I must have missed them 'cause I have such a strong desire to see them again." I said.

56

What a shock it was for me to see Spin and Siri hurrying around the kitchen and then to the eating area. Siri was just a skinny gawky young girl when I last saw her, now she seemed like a young woman, pretty shapely and always smiling. Spin was no doubt a man in every physical sense of the word and almost as tall as myself.

"Hello Spin, hello Siri!" I exclaimed excitedly.

"Good morning dad," they both replied very much as they usually would have done.

"So what's happening today?" I enquired.

"I've got a music test, a recital," said Siri."

"I'm going to the cyber centre to do some extra study on my business ventures. If I get this done today I can hand in my paper at the college and then it will be a short holiday for me, least ways for a month," Spin replied.

"And what business ventures are you up to now," I asked with a profound interest.

"Oh it's just more info-tech work, to get the most out of my soft-ware research." Spin was nonchalant and even blasé.

"You will have to fill me in on it sometime, I'm very interested," I said.

"Well it has nothing to do with marine biology so it's not what does interest you, dad," he said.

"Marine biology?" I replied puzzled.

"All the books and CD ROMs you bring home are to do with marine biology, it seems to have become an obsession with you." Spin seemed slighted that my work took me apart from the family so much. I guessed that was what he was referring to.

"Well I've finished one phase of my work, the initial research, so maybe we could spend a little more time together." I wanted to be with him, get to know him again.

"OK, that's alright with me, thanks dad," he smiled warmly.

I was so amazed with these two offspring, they were mature and their voices were strong and deeper.

I hoped in the future to balance my work and my family responsibilities. I want to feel all of life and not let work dominate what promised to be a very mutually rewarding growth experience for these valued family members.

I felt that I had missed much during my five years absence but I knew also that this time every day mattered, I had a strong sense of purpose; I the extra- terrestrial, alias, Alien X.

57

So here I was, after my transference to planet Earth, within again the able body of Randolph Bilder and eager to pursue a mission that promised to be a great leap forward for earthlings and for the fish people.

However I felt that my efforts would have to be on a relatively small scale at first. Yes, something to do with marine biology and that seemed to be in order considering my heritage and creature interest.

Miriam had to inform me of a new set of personal and work relations. For example my secretary was the same one that my former boss Ralf Putney had had. Her name was Miranda Daily and Miriam told me that Miranda was like Randy's right arm and that she knew personally most of the people with whom I would have work related business. Miriam also told me that Randy had instigated the Holdfast Bay Aqua World project. Randy had gained the approval of the Mayor and most of the City Design Office board, including Ralf Putney who was now a member of the board leaving me to manage the City Design Office on my own. Apparently Randy still worked closely with Rex Gonzales and the Landscape Architect Department's assistant, a young man named Boz Brennon.

The Holdfast Bay Aqua World project was my own baby, my personal obsession as everyone in the Design Office complex well knew. It was Randolph Bilder's idea to fence off with steel netting one of our largest coastal bays and stock it with every known inhabitable fish and marine organism that could live there. It was to be the largest aqua world park in the world not just the Southern Hemisphere. Randolph had been very ambitious, his dream vibrant and an inclusive testament to his visit to my home planet.

Life is life on earth or on my planet and life never stands still, it always evolves, always is in an activity of transformation, of growth and diversification.

58

The following Monday morning I took up residence of my position as Manager of the Design Office. I walked along the corridor of the floor that I only vaguely remembered towards the door of Ralf's former office. There on the door was my sign in large letters:

RANDOLPH BILDER
DESIGN OFFICE MANAGER

I opened the door without knocking, that I supposed was my privilege, and there at the desk sat my secretary Miranda Daily; a woman of near my age dressed in a very business-like dress suit, black pin-stripe on a dark maroon colour. She smiled,

"Morning Randolph," she warmly greeted me.

"Good morning Miranda," I tried to act casual but actually I was quite unsure if I could convince her that I was exactly as I appeared to be; Randolph, calm and my cheerful self.

"You have a busy morning, Ralf is calling in at ten o'clock and a representative of the Tri-Star Corporation has an appointment at one," Miranda was so very business-like it may take a little time to get used to this kind of relatively close associate.

What shall I say.

"Thanks very much Miranda, if there is anything I need I'll tell you later when I think of it, so just have a happy day," I smiled and opened the door to my office.

I let the door swing slowly open and felt the space and light fill my soul. This was a great moment for me, I wanted to remember it and cherish it. It not only symbolized a certain stage in the life of Randy Bilder but I knew it meant power, the power to create; the power to influence.

I strode lightly on the thick carpet to the centre of the office. My desk was large, with flowers and a picture frame. I walked to the other side of the desk and peered at the picture in the frame, it was of Miriam.

"Hello Miriam," I said feeling immensely pleased.

To the door side of the room I looked and saw two large bookshelves on either side of the door. I was yet to realize that these contained most of Randy Bilder's research materials, not only books, large and small, but also CD ROMs, disks, cassettes and assorted maps and magazines. He had apparently devoted himself to *this* marine research and as I was to find out, our destinies were tied, my future had become his, and we breathed as one, in this room the sky office.

59

"Good morning Ralf," said I as the imposing though friendly form of my former manager entered my office.

"Hi there, Randolph. Good to see you, and how are things with you?" said Ralf cheerily. "Very well, Ralf; come over here and have a seat. We both sat in the two large armchairs.

"I must thank you again for keeping me on as a casual consultant, I really look forward to our monthly meetings," he said.

"Your help is keeping me going and I like seeing you too, only I wish we could play golf more often." I tried to encourage his friendliness.

"Well we are both busy men, but if you want to make that once a month it's fine with me. And how is Miriam?" said Ralf.

"Yes I'd like a monthly game thanks. And yes Miriam is exceptionally well." I replied.

He stood up then and walked slowly around the perimeter of the room. On the bookshelves he stared intently at several framed photographs. As I approached I saw that they were of the Putney Bridge and the West Park statue.

"I still don't know how you did it! " He started on a new tack. "You know you will have my support with the board for any proposal but how did you get the Mayor on side for such a fantastic project as the Holdfast Bay Aqua World?" He paused, but before I could reply he spoke, "I suspect that Spin had something to do with it. He has been dating the Mayor's grand-daughter for the last three years and now it looks like you're actually going to be related to the Mayor. What a charming co-incidence."

I was very surprised. What could I possibly say to *this?*

"Well I've heard rumours but Spin has been quite secretive about the whole matter," I bluffed.

"Oh well, luck has its ways but how lucky can you be?" he paused again and his eyebrows twitched.

We stepped back to the armchairs and sat again.

"So everything is set for the first stage of the Bay development. It was very useful to use the Boron/Mercury process for the entire construction. And how is Tri-Star managing the transportation?" He wasn't aware but this was the first I had heard of it.

"Oh I'm meeting with them this afternoon just after lunch so I could let you know of any developments." I had to at least appear knowledgeable.

"I thought they were the best for the job and lucky again that Pamela is the assistant manager of Tri-Star." He continued to surprise me.

"Pamela, assistant manager, is that right?" said I.

"Yes not only is Spin a going concern with Pamela, you know the Mayor's grand-daughter, but now the commercial bond is being fixed with Tri-Star." Ralf was relaxed but I was ruffled; *so much* I didn't know.

I decided it would be wise to change the subject so I said, "And how is Shiree these days."

"Oh wonderful and Mia is a fine daughter only she is showing signs of obsessive behaviour." He beamed proudly.

"Oh really, what kind of obsessive behaviour?" I continued on with great interest.

"She seems to want to swim all the time, the beach the pool, hot weather or cold she's in it. If we tell her to ease off she cries and gets very upset. We don't know what to make of it."

"Yes obsessive, rather strange but perhaps it's just a phase she's going through. I remember that Spin was interested in punk music when he was younger; played his CD's all the time. We were worried but he's grown out of it. So I wouldn't be too worried. Just give it time." I found it easy to give advice as I had found it easy to encourage others. But I was quite intrigued with this new trait of Shiree's and my child.

Ralf and I continued our consultation for another half hour and then he departed leaving me with a fixed date for our next game of golf.

60

So here I am back in my home city, I called it home now. As I looked out of my windows or walls as it were, I thought of Brookland, a much bigger city with much taller buildings. I looked into the distance at suburbs stretching away in every direction. I looked at buildings nearby and smaller than the Design Office building, and I looked down at people on the streets. My mind seemed to be blank except for thoughts of Mia and her obsession, an unusual one for earthlings.

My mind then focussed on this Tri-Star Corporation business, something about transport. What could it have to do with an Aqua World complex? Well I thought people would be there looking around presumably, and they may need to travel quite a distance, but how?

It wasn't long and an executive from Tri-Star entered my office. He introduced himself, and we sat and talked for two hours. His company was one of the largest in the Southern Hemisphere. His company had planned the movements of thousands of people every day in this Aqua World of Holdfast Bay.

The complex covered the entire bay area in three parts and these parts were linked by pathways that allowed for three types of movement of people. People were to walk on one path; ride bicycles, roller blades or skates on another, and the third was a mini-train; a rail track that slowly took people from one end of the complex to another in a circular circuit.

As the base area had been dredged and cleared and the steel net fence erected, it was now that Tri-Star had to move in and position equipment and barges to begin the linking of kiosk centres in each part of the complex. The Tri-Star executive informed me of the time factor and the need to begin placing the tunnels made of clear boron/mercury material that linked the whole complex.

It was exciting stuff. Randy had done well with the assistance of the Landscape Architects Department and Rex Gonzales.

I went home early with a lot to think of. I commuted along the auto way with Diana Kraul still playing on the CD player, as though time had stood still. And what better place to stand still, moving quickly along the auto way towards the cool darkening evening sky.

61

The next week passed quickly as I learnt of the goings on in my absence. I had a game of golf with Spin and he told me that his affair with Pamela was quite serious; they had met at the opening ceremony of the West Park statue. Apparently they intended marrying within six months and to live in Brookland.

Miriam told me a wondrous story about the fish people. Randy had arrived on the planet around the mating season when the fish people felt compelled to propagate for three months of the year, one year of their time being about the length of two earth years.

The fish people were not monogamous and merely swam near each other, males and females touching and releasing eggs and sperm that quickly fertilized and grew into baby fish children. They did not leave the water until puberty although they always mated under water.

Randolph changed all that and chose his mates as he knew them and only copulated on land in a more human fashion. In fact he set the fashion trend and millions of fish people now choose their mates and do the act on land. The fish people only lived for approximately forty earth years and were considered old after thirty years where-upon they usually stayed in the water.

The fish people also had food farms for other fish and vegetable marine matter, and they had huge banquets of a communal nature in the shallows of the shores of their oceans. They were the highest of intelligence of creatures on their planet, being, so Randy had said, somewhere between dolphins and humans in their development.

All this was fascinating to me and I hoped that Randy was having a rewarding experience. Miriam said laughingly that Randy had plans to construct millions of individually styled mating cubicles near the beaches of the fish planet. Well, I thought, wonders never cease. It would not be a wonder if it didn't change, evolve or lead onto something else. As usual it was all flux and flow in our ever-changing universe

I worked steadily, studying, absorbing, cross referencing and collating information from the comprehensive materials that Randy had collected in his sky office. Through actual marine biology with references to the major ocean types of fishes, to oceanographic and tidal information I waded for many months and I found I had not unnaturally a kind of predestined inclination for studying this marine life and marine environment data. There were moments sometimes days when I let my mind wander not being able to concentrate on such an involving subject at all times. I did get the idea fixed in my head that I should try to find out more about my home planet. Having a space observatory nearby it seemed obvious to satisfy my curiosity.

One day when the rain poured down steadily I called the space observatory and spoke to an astronomer named John Trummer. He made an appointment for me to visit on the next fine night, he said, someone would call to confirm it. Maybe I could find the current state of research into my planet or at least my part of the sky. From the depths of the ocean to the furthest depths of outer-space my curiosity strove onwards, purposefully, rewardingly; if only every human life could be so fulfilling I thought.

The days sped by with great pleasure on the one hand, as I drove to work in the rain; it rained continuously for two weeks and there were floods in the nearby countryside, but I was warm and cosseted inside the air-conditioned car; and on the other hand, I had to wait to visit the space observatory.

But at home each night it was pure joy, I no longer studied at home but gave myself to the family, playing table games and learning to be quite a good cook as Randy had been.

It was on one such evening when I drifted without a care into a dark cold night that I sat chatting with Miriam and Siri.

"And I've found that if I buy the cosmetics that are on special I can get a free gift. It's not the main line of the shop but it's free. I've gotten eye-liner and make up, perfume and talk powder all for free." Siri was sure she was getting a bargain.

"But you have to remember that the cheaper or free products are not always good for your skin or your hair. I know lots of women who have used cheap products when they were younger and in a few years they had wrinkles and pallid looking skin and lank colourless hair, it's better not to use the cheap stuff - better sometimes to pass up the bargains and choose the established brands or you may regret this experimentation in a few years." Miriam was so wise, wiser than most men and women and such a great asset.

Many a night did I spend with Miriam and Spin or Siri; it was pure joy. Family life has great advantages.

All was going well with the Holdfast Bay Aqua World project. The first stage was almost complete and the marine specialists were assembling the greatest assortment of marine life ever seen on earth. This menagerie would attract tourists, professionals even, from all over the world. My associates on the board and the Mayor were very pleased that another world class asset was being added to my city's attractions; in fact my city was even rivalling the thriving metropolis of Brookland.

I wasn't surprised during a lull in the construction of the bay project to get a call from the space observatory. I could visit that night at one o'clock, this being the best time for observing.

I was met by John Trummer at the reception desk and he led me into a large room containing computers and video screens.

"Now, just what was it you were wanting to look at," he said cheerily.

"A star a long way from earth that I first noticed many years ago. It seemed different in colour from other stars and I have been fascinated with this particular star," I explained.

"North, south, east or west," he said smiling.

"Well as I remember it was kind of north east but close to the centre of the sky, and it seemed to be very distant." I had only a vague memory of the position of the star.

"OK," said John, "let's bring up that area." He turned, pressed some buttons on a panel and a view of the stars appeared on a large screen above us.

"Well I'm not sure," I stared questioningly. "It seems that that cluster of galaxies to the right was just above a smaller more distant group of stars."

"OK, let's home in a little closer," he said as he pressed a key on a row of buttons. The image on the screen immediately expanded and passed the first cluster of galaxies on the right settling then on the small group. He pressed another button and the view expanded again until it was possible to see several solar systems superimposed on each other.

"Which one does it look like to you?" He looked at me with a deepening interest.

I stared for some moments at the screen. "Could you put it on a smaller screen at eye level and focus on the third solar system just on the left, please John."

John reached to another panel of buttons and pressed one, the view above disappeared and the image simultaneously appeared on a monitor in front of us at eye level.

I stared again for some moments until I thought I could distinguish a faint yellow haze on the left.

"Could you focus on this area," I said, pointing to the appropriate zone of the screen.

"Yes I can do that," he smiled and pressed another button on one of the panels.

The screen took a framed view of the zone and then expanded it again. I could clearly see the exact solar system now and the third planet from it's sun was definitely of a yellow colour.

"This planet here," I said, "that seems to be the one."

"Let's see the location now," he said typing some data on a keyboard. He pressed some more buttons and some data came on view on another monitor nearby. "Nearly," he said, typing some more on the keyboard. "Yes," he said, "that's it," and he looked at the screen as though I might be able to tell him something.

"It's just figures, numbers, to me," I said looking also at the screen.

He typed some more on the keyboard and some names appeared on the screen.

I read, "Stussy-Oberon Complex."

"It's the Stussy-Oberon Complex," said John as he typed some more data in.

I read from the screen, "Discovery - Maxine Stussy and Simon Oberon 1986 - Santa Catalina Observatory, Argentina."

"You see what the solar system is called, who discovered it and when," said John.

"Anymore information on that particular star," I enquired.

He typed more data into the system and more information appeared on the screen.

"Space probe 1996 - reports planet Oberon, is twice size of Earth and has atmosphere that could support life. Half land, half ocean. Yellow glow caused by estimated apparent afferent centres in lower troposphere. Recommend further investigation. U.N. space programme - 2004."

"Very interesting," said John, "it's amazing that you could locate just *that* particular planet. Quite amazing!

65

Amazed at the technical abilities of the observatory and John Trummer I wasn't. I was astounded! The technological expertise on this planet, planet Earth was beyond my comprehension, but then again most earthlings would not know just how a television works or how nuclear energy is generated but these things were what life on this planet depended on.

In so many fields professionals had knowledge that was so specialized that individual scientists could not speak the same language as other scientists or the average person. Computerisation apparently speeds the processes of research so that what would have taken a lifetime of research by a large team of investigators can now be achieved by one or two scientists, although part of a global community, in about ten years.

I believed that humanity had control of its destiny, could direct cultural and technological evolution. I then found that I was not so curious about so many things that I saw everyday in the natural environment and what I was aware of as part of the cultural inheritance of humankind. Like reading an encyclopaedia there was so much that wasn't personally useful.

"I will stick to my marine research," I reassured myself, "Yes my life has a purpose!"

66

Time marched ever onwards at an unstoppable pace as I delved deeper into the world under the oceans of planet Earth. I knew their extent, their depth, and I read articles of deep oceanographic research.

I became aware of the hierarchy of intelligence of marine creatures. I read extensively of the edible fishes and those that were of use to humans for innumerable purposes. I read of aqua-business and fish farming, the major companies and I read of dolphins.

My curiosity about dolphins was immense, I wanted to know everything about them for they were I surmised the closest oceanic fish to those to whom I belonged on planet Oberon.

I tried not to be obsessive and managed to play many games of golf; to be with Spin, Ralf and sometimes with the Landscape Architecture Supervisor, Rex Gonzalez. We talked of many things during our games and I was very appreciative of their divulgences about other people. I was more than interested in social interaction; what was happening with their families and friends as well as why some things happened, just as they did. My friends took many things for granted but the most trivial humorous event made me laugh perhaps when it wasn't appropriate. They thought I was very caring and sensible to themselves in a personal way, they sometimes would say this.

I also liked to gaze at the clouds, and watch the birds as though they were doing the impossible. Planes flew overhead sometimes but I didn't think twice about people up there above the clouds, but the birds, they were a great wonder, an endless source of fascination.

I seemed to be drifting on a directed wave of good fortune, as if nothing could now influence the trajectory of my life's continual growth and renewal.

67

It was six months into my visit to Earth that I, Alien X became aware of a new force in my life.

Miriam Daily, my secretary, appeared every few days now with faxes from Singapore.

The South Asian Alliance Construction Company who were contracted to build the Holdfast Bay project wanted me to visit a representative in Brookland. The company said that they had future contracts for various projects; fish farming and storage facilities as well as cable laying and oceanographic research, and they wanted my consultancy. They also wanted exclusive rights to use the boron/mercury process for their projects in the South Asian region.

I wasn't concerned in the least, at first, and faxed back to them that I would consider their offers. They were persistent and finally they said that I could meet with a representative of Global Monarch Incorporated, the parent multi-national to discuss the future prospects for the whole planet as far as Global Monarch was concerned.

It was an unusual initiative for a large company of that size. When I sought Ralf's advice he said I should definitely meet with the representative. I thought about it a few days more and then Ralf suggested I take a legal councillor, a member of the board with me to a meeting.

I didn't feel ready at this stage to pursue the offer but Ralf said that the board would pay for the trip so it seemed like a bit of a holiday, a journey of fun, leisure and a bit of the high life. So finally I accepted.

68

There was something uncanny about this trip to Brookland. I had been there many times, at least, Randy Bilder had, but this time I felt I could easily get out of my depth: too far from my known surroundings where a high flying fast efficient business executive could lead me astray onto paths that I could not comprehend at that point.

Therefore wary as I was I wanted to feel grounded, to have some one familiar to me nearby. Consequently I asked Spin to go with me. He could have a lot of free time on his own, fun in the big city and maybe do some personal business. He was very enthusiastic and agreed without much consideration.

We set out a week later, cruising along the auto way in the rain, in a taxi and feeling a spirit of mutual camaraderie; boys on the town sort of thing, a little adventure that we could share and keep as a memory. Spin had three months until he was to be married to Pamela so this was an opportunity for us, perhaps the last, to be together as father and son, deepening the filial bond as I feel the real Randolph Bilder would want us to do.

We sat together on the plane, the lawyer adviser that Ralf had recommended had a seat further away. We were all staying at the Mirador Hotel. I had the penthouse suite again of which one room was to be Spin's. The lawyer stayed in another part of the hotel. We had lunch in the Mirador Hotel restaurant, Spin and myself, delicious food and I didn't have to wash any dishes.

I didn't know at this point that this event was a turning point in the life of Randy Bilder and very important for Alien X as well. Soon I would not be washing dishes anymore or doing any other household chores. My life style would undergo a change from medium size city public professional to more worldly concerns. As I had a purpose although I wasn't sure what that purpose was, I was willing to change, to adapt and to grow.

That after noon I had a briefing with the board's lawyer in a private lounge of the Mirador Hotel. Spin went looking for accommodations for himself and Pamela to move into after their marriage.

The lawyer was officious and stern. An older man with a life-time of experience behind him, he first advised me that he had to protect the interests of Rex Gonzalez as to the boron/mercury copyright. He also advised me to make no decisions; to defer all questions and requests, to sign nothing and to refer to himself on any matter of uncertainty. He said that apparently this was a formal introduction to the medium league of corporate management and Global Monarch would try to tempt me away from public spirited concerns into the realms of high business finance where profit maximization would be the first priority.

The meeting lasted an hour only, the lawyer instructing me to be at a certain business office at ten o'clock the next morning where the meeting would take place.

69

Spin arrived back at the penthouse suite in the evening and said he had found a house for Pamela and himself. He said he would be going night-clubbing later, would I like to join him. I said I had to rest and get my brain in peak form for my meeting. We sat in the hotel lounge and had a few drinks from the bar. We talked for several hours and had an evening meal in the dining area.

Spin said that this may be his last time to be on the town without Pamela and being in Brookland he wanted this night to be a kind of right of passage, to end one phase of his life and begin another. Also this being a very open town he thought he could find a woman to spend the night with, at least he could say to Pamela that he had experience.

What an experience for us both we were yet to know, for the most significant events can grow from innocent little seeds.

70

Early the next morning I heard a knocking on my bedroom door, it was Spin and he was eager to tell me that he had met an exciting girl in a disco. He had brought her to his room and they had made love. The girl left only half an hour earlier and Spin felt that she had made a man of him.

He said that the girl's name was Jennifer Poute who was known as Jenny Poute when she was in Paris. She had divulged that she was the daughter of a business lawyer and her grand-father was Managing Director of a large multi-national company. Spin had been approached by the girl and he was attracted to her from the first. It was her suggestion that they spend the night together.

I asked if he would be seeing her again and Spin said that they had exchanged phone numbers but the girl had said "Don't call me, I'll call you."

Spin then went out to do some shopping and I prepared myself for my meeting.

I arrived at precisely 10 o'clock at the business office where the meeting was to take place. Written on the door in large print was the sign:

GLOBAL MONARCH INCORPORATED

A secretary sat at a desk in a large lobby area, my lawyer associate sat at a centre table drinking coffee. It was not long to wait, I had a coffee, and then a door opened, a tall man with glasses came out, shook hands with us and said he was simply, "Stanley", the representative of Global Monarch.

In his large luxurious office time passed quickly and soon two hours had disappeared. The lawyer, Stanley had explained that Global Monarch was interested in an exclusive rights contract for utilization of the boron/mercury process, a joint contract with Rex Gonzalez and I. Global Monarch was offering an unprecedented amount of money, stock options and openings to positions on boards in their subsidiary companies. It had construction possibilities all over the planet and Global Monarch wanted to finalize a deal as soon as possible.

My lawyer associate explained that Rex would have to be advised as he had previous commitments that may be with companies that were in competition with Global Monarch subsidiaries. If any agreement could be made this factor would have to be accommodated as the City Board had an interest in the honouring of Rex's contracts.

I said I would need more details before making any counter proposal or decision.

The company representative said that additional details would be faxed to me personally. My lawyer insisted that he also receive a faxed copy of the details and internet addresses etc. were given.

It was a smooth operation for us all I thought and opened new possibilities for myself.

I caught a taxi back to the Mirador Hotel stopping a few blocks before we arrived there. As I walked on this fine autumn day I observed the buildings and particularly the people. People who had plans and dreams, people who were not aware that large multi- national companies like Global Monarch were setting the scene for their adventures, providing a means for them to discover just what it is in themselves that makes a human a human and in my case an alien an extra-terrestrial.

71

I was relaxing in the penthouse suite; the meeting had been a success with no mistakes on my part. It seemed that a strain had been put upon me; I felt tiredness throughout my body and I hadn't realized that negotiating on such a meaningful level could deplete my physical energy to such a degree.

I lay on the lounge intending to have a short nap but Spin breezed in, a ball of energy. Oh to be younger, I thought; although the life of a fish person was much shorter than a human, according to Randy's account, I felt that I was still reasonably young and should be lively and capable of activity at all times.

Spin mixed a drink at the lounge bar and told me how he had found bargains in the galleries, pictures that he really liked, at a good price. He could see that I was tired so he sat and seemed to be thinking. I was just drifting off into a pleasant doze when Spin's mobile phone rang. He answered and it was Jennifer Poute.

Jennifer asked him to go to the window and look at the building opposite, another hotel. She said she was on a balcony on the eighteenth floor. Spin searched down and saw a figure in white waving.

"I can see her," he said.

"Maybe you can see better with these," I said, getting a pair of binoculars out of a cupboard and giving them to Spin. They were provided by the hotel.

He said that was much better. I had a look through the binoculars at the balcony and I could see a very young, very pretty girl. I handed the binoculars back to Spin. He could see Jennifer clearly now as she waved and asked him if he wanted to see a movie at a cinema.

"Which movie?" asked Spin. James Bond replied Jennifer. "James Bond, great!" exclaimed Spin.

Before he left Spin told me excitedly that Jennifer was one of the wealthiest girls in the world for her age.

"How old is she," I asked.

"Eighteen," he said.

"And what is this big multi-national her family is involved with," I enquired curiously.

"Global Monarch," he replied.

So it was that Spin left soon after to see the movie with Jennifer and I thought I could now have my nap. I was drifting off again on the lounge when my mobile phone rang.

"Randolph Bilder please," a female voice said.

"Speaking," I replied.

"I believe that your son Spin has gone to a movie with my daughter, Jennifer. Is that true?"

"Yes, that's correct," I replied.

"Well I have to tell you something about Jennifer. By the way I am on the balcony of the eighteenth floor of the building opposite, can you see me?" she said.

I quickly picked up the binoculars and focused on the balcony. There she was, a very beautiful older version of Jennifer.

"Yes I see you," said I.

She waved and said, "Can I come over to visit you about a certain matter concerning Jennifer?"

"Why, er .. yes, that would be fine," I answered her.

So she got my room number and said goodbye until later.

I was unprepared for all this. Firstly Jennifer, being very rich and her family involvement with Global Monarch and now her mother apparently wanting to divulge family secrets, there seemed too much of a coincidence about this incident. If Jennifer's grand-father was the Managing Director of Global Monarch and Global Monarch wanted me to sign a huge contract worth millions, it all seemed a bit suspect.

72

Jennifer's mother entered the penthouse suite with a vivacious sweep of her long fur coat.

"Hi, I'm Kate," she announced, "Kate Poute, I am the mother of that precocious teenager you saw on the balcony this afternoon. You did see her didn't you?"

39

"Yes I saw her and yourself as you know," I replied.

"Well what did you think of her, beautiful, yeh?" She said with a wave of her arm.

"Oh yes very pretty," said I.

"Like her mother don't you think," she said.

"Yes very like her mother," I replied.

Kate looked around the penthouse suite, "Very nice," she said, "but *my,* isn't it hot in here? Mind if I take my coat off?"

"Of course," I said as I took her coat and hung it in the hallway. As I came back, I was stunned. She was wearing a little school girl's tunic tied at the waist, and it was transparent; there was nothing underneath the tunic.

"Now I have to tell you and your son to be wary of Jennifer. She makes up stories. Oh yes! She has a million fantasies." Kate walked the length of the room like a model, very flirtatiously I would say.

"So don't go believing any stories about her and I being rich and related to managers of big businesses. We are just a widow and daughter from the suburbs of Brookland; we are in fact quite poor. We just wanted one weekend in a five star hotel and we don't even have enough money to pay the bill." She paused stepping close to me and smiled.

"Actually," she said "I was wondering if you could lend me a few hundred dollars just to tide us over." She winked and said, "I would be ever so grateful."

I tried to calm myself but I was becoming increasingly excited by this woman who shocked with every movement, every word. I stepped over to the lounge bar. "Can I fix us a drink," I said.

"Yes, cognac for me," she said.

"Sorry no alcohol, would you like a coke and ice," said I.

"Oh! Yes! Coke and ice, my favourite," she stood with her hands on her hips, provocatively. I found I had an erection.

"Now don't go getting ideas," she did pout. "But if you do there is a bedroom nearby I suppose, isn't there?"

"Oh yes there is a bedroom and I am getting ideas. I must say I find you extremely provocative and exciting."

She strode forcefully to me and kissed me with no uncertainty of intention. We kissed for a long, long time then she whispered, "If you want to go into the bedroom now that's fine with me." She laughed, shaking her long brown hair, "actually I'd really enjoy it." As I pressed my lips upon her milk-white breasts, I thought, *for only this, I always want to be a human*. Then we kissed for another age until I could stand it no longer and I led her into the bedroom.

She was a riot, I remember. One of the best encounters of an intimate nature I was ever to have as an alien. Also I was sure even Randy Bilder himself could not have had such a thrilling seduction in all his years.

As she slipped on her fur coat she patted my cheek, "Now please don't forget that I and my daughter are actually quite poor so I'm reminding you; could you lend us a couple of hundred. I'll give it back next time you're in Brookland, just give me a call if you want a quickie."

I handed over the two hundred dollars thinking, if this isn't normal behaviour it probably should be.

Then I went to bed for the deepest night's sleep an earthling could hope for.

73

Back in my sky room; the City Design Managers Office, and after a few days, I found myself very tired even physically exhausted. I was tired of wading through scientific books, and the videos of earthly fish creatures although interesting were hardly stimulating.

I felt I needed to get out of this room for a while, to be more active. With this in mind I visited the site of construction of the Holdfast Bay Aqua World. The project was in advance of my expectations, the first stage had been completed and the waters had been stocked with many marine creatures. The first kiosk was now built and the transport pathways had been constructed. I entered the tunnel from a ramp and the walkway dipped down under the seawater. The water was bright with light and clear enough to see many hundreds of small fish of various kinds. I saw strange creatures, transparent with tentacles floating down and fish that I knew were sting rays. Some fishes were multi-coloured, some were slow moving and others darted quickly about.

As I walked, stopping occasionally to view some fish or creature, I became aware of larger fish near the surface. They were jumping out of the water and then diving close to the side of the tunnel. Then it was that I found a name for them, yes, these are dolphins, I said to myself. I watched them twist here and dart there, jump and then dive. They were playful creatures and I could vaguely hear their bubbly cries permeating to me, through the waters and through the tunnel's walls.

It must have been an hour before I was aware that I had been listening to them. They had been talking in a communal, group mind kind of way. I knew that they were hungry and that the water was too warm for them. Only Alien X, could understand dolphins; I, a fish person in the depths of my soul. I was sure I could do something to help them.

I walked onwards seeing many more marine creatures but I could not understand any noises that issued from them. I came to the kiosk where I ordered a coffee and a waiter brought me a hot, soothing strong mug of coffee. The ocean environment surrounded me and I felt somewhat at home and relaxed. The tension of the previous few days eased away from me as I stared above at the light from the surface.

A man of about my age approached the table, "Hello, I'm the marine supervisor, and you I believe are Randolph Bilder from the City Design Office."

I affirmed this and we got into a conversation about the Aqua World progress and about the three zones where the various marine creatures were to have their homes. He said, amongst other things, that the three zones were of differing depths and the waters were kept at constant temperatures except for seasonal adjustments. I suggested that perhaps allowances should be made for the fish to adjust themselves and that in fact right now the water in this zone could be too warm for them. He said he hadn't considered that and that he would speak to the environmental manager about it. If more allowance for the creatures adjustments to the temperature themselves was to be made this would certainly be taken into account in the settings of the temperatures.

I then caught the mini-train back to the shore and as I walked along the beach I saw a small jetty with a landing platform. On the landing platform was a man who was emptying bags into the water and throwing pieces of, it looked like fish pieces, into the water. I was wanting to know what he was doing so I strolled out on the jetty and as I approached the man stopped and looked up at me.

"Good afternoon," I said. Then I said, "are you feeding the fish?"

"Yes," he replied, "they don't get all the food that they need naturally in these waters; they need a supplement." "At this early point in their introduction do you think there is enough naturally occurring food sources for the fish, for example the dolphins; it may take time to build a sizable pool of sources to feed on. I was very concerned about the dolphins in particular."

"They may need some extra natural food sources, you're right, it's early days yet and if time hasn't allowed for the smaller fish to multiply we'll have to supply more of them. I'll check it out," he said co-operatively. "And as the fish, the dolphins in particular have only been in this new environment for a short time maybe they haven't acclimatized yet, maybe they feel disorientated and anxious and get hungrier than they usually would." I wanted so much that the fish should feel comfortable in their new home.

"That maybe so, I could certainly increase the dolphins' supplementary portion to some extent, I would like them to adjust to this bay as soon as possible," he paused. "Are you a professional or something, you seem to know what you're talking about."

"I'm very interested in the fish," I said. "My name is Randolph Bilder; Manager of the City Design Office."

74

Into my second week of being very tired everyday, I was usually exhausted and physically depleted of energy by lunchtime each day. I decided I had to do something about the situation so I asked Miriam what was the best thing to do and she said to pay a visit to the family doctor. I was a bit concerned that the doctor may want me to have x-rays of my head or brain scans but this concern was unwarranted. The doctor simply advised me to get more exercise, he said to workout in a gymnasium once a week and to take an evening walk everyday.

This was not a problem for me. I found the gym an interesting experience and doing weights quite exciting. My evening walks which I took to like a fish to water were a delight because, living in an outer suburb I only had to walk for ten minutes and I was into the countryside. Miriam felt it would be good for her too so she came with me. We walked passed very tall trees and open pastoral land where there were sheep and cows.

As the sun was setting each evening we walked for about an hour along country lanes that were very beautiful and tranquil. We also saw many *brilliant* sun-sets. On these walks we talked of many things and I found myself in a state of being as I imagined the real Randy Bilder would have been. We spoke of love and how earthlings usually mated for life and how strange it seemed to Miriam that the fish people had had to be shown how to even make love as couples on the sunny shores of my home planet.

I told her of my discovery, of the name and details of my planet after visiting the Space Observatory. Oberon, it sounded strong and noble but what was it really like? What was the real Randolph experiencing right at that moment, as a fish person in a strange world?

As we returned from our walk each night the darkened night sky gleamed with stars but I was unable to identify my star, my Oberon.

75

I received the details of the proposals of Global Monarch Incorporated. I slowly perused the bulky document that I had had my secretary, Miranda print out copies of from the messages on the computer. There were many options and the bulk sum of the amount of money offered was astounding. Also I was offered stock options in Global Monarch and many of it's subsidiaries. There were fourteen companies I could become a board member of. I was interested in two of them; Pacific Extensive Pty. Ltd., and Deep Sea Explorations Worldwide Corporation. I had Miranda check their details and she returned to me with extra information on these two companies.

Pacific Extensive had wide ranging interests, from mining to cable laying and fishing. Deep Sea Explorations was concerned with exploring and mapping the deeper parts of the earth's oceans. I was very interested and I felt they had potential, I wasn't sure *what* potential at that point, but perhaps I could do something with them.

The question of the boron/mercury process rights was something that I would have to wait on, although I wanted to go ahead, I couldn't see how Rex Gonzales could compromise his position. I therefore believed that we would have to have separate contracts.

76

I had been worried lately on two counts; firstly the so called "apparent afferent centres" in the lower troposphere of the planet Oberon seemed to imply something ominous, something not wholly keeping to the initial innocence of a simple fishy planet. I did want to know more about what they could possibly be.

Secondly, I was concerned with this person, Jennifer Poute. Was she fibbing? How could she have a connection to Global Monarch Incorporated? It was all too much of a coincidence. However as it was all so unable to be checked I let these reoccurring worries drift on without doing anything about them.

Time has a way of ameliorating our most nagging uncertainties and doubts, I felt, either I would get to the bottom of these incongruities or I would forget them. I promised myself not to worry, and if I did continue for some time to feel concern I believed this was only natural, only human.

77

At this time I took to visiting the Holdfast Bay Aqua World site every morning, interesting myself in the construction and the fish. What with this, going to the gym and my evening walks I was feeling much better, much fitter.

The second zone was gradually nearing completion and at this early stage fish were already being released into the bowl of the zone. I always walked to the kiosk of the first zone and caught the mini-train back to the shore. The dolphins were getting used to me and always swam near. They now seemed to be contented in their new home.

I had long conversations with the marine supervisor and the environmental manager as well as lesser officials. We spoke of the functions of the three zones, how each represented a certain ecological niche in the wide ocean outside the bay, and in other parts of the world. The marine supervisor inspired my imagination with talk of the octopi, the large octopi, which were going to be placed in the third zone. I was certainly looking forward to seeing them. A site manager said that all three zones would be completed within six months and the entire complex then opened to the public. It was expected that there would be tourists and general public visitors numbering in the hundreds of thousands every year.

I now felt ready to contemplate further afield, on the wide blue oceans of planet earth.

78

Another month of relative calm passed, uneventful and giving me time to relax and contemplate the ocean's deep through the medium of my books and videos in the sky office.

One morning after my visit to the Aqua World site Miranda handed me a large faxed message. It was from Rex Gonzales. He had negotiated to keep his options open and his interests intact. He did not agree to the exclusive right to the use of the boron/mercury process for Global Monarch, instead he opted for a more limited agreement and a contract which gave him roughly half as much money as I would be getting and no positions on boards. He preferred to align stock options with his other interests and this left him free to pursue any possibilities with smaller building contractors who often had more public-spirited interests.

I was now free to complete a deal with Global Monarch on my own terms. I would agree to exclusive rights to Global Monarch. I wanted a position on the board of Pacific Extensive and also on the board of Deep Sea Explorations. Besides this I wanted stock options for a large percentage of these two companies' shares.

I discussed my preferences with Ralf and with the board's lawyer and we drew up a contract which was faxed to Global Monarch Incorporated.

A week later Miranda advised me to go to the video conference room for a meeting with the Managing Director of Global Monarch. I entered the room for the first time, it was to be my first experience of video conferencing. A technician sat me down in front of a large video screen alongside which was a camera focussed on my face and shoulders. I could see my image on the screen and the technician moved me and told me to raise my head to get the best picture of my face.

Then a picture of the Managing Director came on the screen. He was an older man, approximately sixty-five years of age, I estimated. He was wearing glasses with thick tortuous shell rims. He asked if I was receiving his voice and seeing his image. I said yes, and then he smiled,

"Welcome aboard the Global Monarch Corporation. My name is Albert Poute, I am the Managing Director of Global Monarch Incorporated. As you can see by our name we have ambition and we have the power to achieve that ambition. We are an incorporated company that means that the aims of the company are those of its members. Although Global Monarch has a large proportion of public stock and shares our aims are the ambitions of its executive, we form a separate legal entity. In accepting your offer we are proposing that you share your talents, your resources with the other managers who compose the corporation. The offer is of course like-wise, Global Monarch offers you the talents and expertise of the management team. In short your goals are ours and our goals to the extent of your willingness are yours. We co-operate as a corporate team not the least of our aims being the maximization of profit and the exploitation of resources, firstly to satisfy the aims of the team and then the needs of the shareholders.

I will personally be sending you a letter of congratulations and the corporation will send you a wealth of information about how to utilize the resources of the company. The contract that you propose will be legally approved and constituted and returned to you as soon as possible. Thank you from myself and my family. Thank you Randolph Bilder".

79

I received the information from Global Monarch within the next few days and the letter of congratulations from Albert Poute soon after.

"Albert Poute," I said and thought. So perhaps what Jennifer Poute had said was true and what her mother had said was a falsification, some kind of cover-up for Jennifer's divulgences. The mystery was deepening.

If Kate Poute was married to a Global Monarch business lawyer and his father was actually Albert Poute how was it that she could say what she did; do what she did. I was completely mystified, the episode had little influence on my signing with Global Monarch but what significance could it have for the future? Corporate intrigue at this early stage was unexpected but if I could come to terms with these events and somehow assimilate them then I felt I would be a better, stronger person.

Global Monarch Incorporated itself was basically a massive construction company with projects on every continent and it had designs on all the ocean regions. One thing that elevated Global Monarch above the ordinary was it's tendency to own the land and property on which it's constructions were built. It was a major world property owner with extensive interests in transport networks. Many public and world famous edifices were either built buy Global Monarch in the form of it's subsidiaries or the land on which they were built was owned by them, or both. The list was endless, the land on which the Eiffel Tower and the Empire State building and even the land on which the pylons of the Sydney Harbour bridge stood was at least fifty percent owned by Global Monarch. The company's designs were great and extensive. I was very impressed by the league that I was entering. At the same time I believed the monopolizing effect of Global Monarch could be a positive or negative attribute. I was a little afraid that one day I may be constricted by this power although I had the vision to see that, my aims being well intentioned, I could achieve very much with this type of power at my finger-tips.

Was I getting too ambitious? Not according to Albert Poute. But what would be my next step; what was I hoping to achieve; and what did Alien X have as an ultimate aim. At this time I had only an inkling of what was to come, but I knew also that great things, magnificent things would be the result of Randolph Bilder's first step on the corporate ladder.

81

The second zone of the Holdfast Bay Aqua World was almost complete. I had seen the construction from many points of view around the bay and from under the water. I had also had the operations explained to me by the various supervisors. It was amazing what large machinery could achieve in a short time. I was very pleased with the progress.

The afternoons I spent in the Design Office were a mixture of pure absorption in the books there or idle indistinct times of daydreaming as I looked at the clouds' changing shapes, dissolving and reforming into each other.

On one such afternoon Miranda entered the room with a message. The astronomer, John Trummer from the space observatory would like to see me about an urgent matter.

I arrived at the observatory later that same day and John showed me into his office.

"We have received a message from the planet Oberon, actually it was received at Sun Valley Observatory, California. It was addressed to you; attention Randolph Bilder. I am reporting this to you confidentially; we don't want this to become public knowledge. A certain Professor Geiger at the Dusseldorf Institute translated the coded message from ultra-violet vibrations," said John.

Codename: Mr Alien, the message was :

Prepare Holdfast third zone for gametes of sub-specie. Directive - Cloud Spirit People. Congratulations RB.

John Trummer was calm when he said, "Why do you think you would be getting a message from planet Oberon."

"Perhaps I am of use to some extra-terrestrials," I said. "They seem to know about my work and want to send some *gametes* to Earth to go in the third zone of Holdfast Aqua World. I suppose I had better prepare for receiving them. But it does seem amazing to me." I tried to remain calm as well.

"This message of course is unprecedented. We, the U.N. affiliated association of alien phenomena, will have to begin an investigation, perhaps send a landing craft to Oberon," said John.

"Yes, of course we must find out about life on other planets. And I am curious about these *gametes*. Something to do with propagating various sub-species from Oberon on earth. So apparently there is a higher species directing this operation. And what do you make of the name, *Cloud Spirit People*," said I.

"It seems to be related to the detection of the afferent centres in the lower troposphere of Oberon. We will have to wait for the investigation," John said, smiling to calm me.

"We will keep you informed of any developments of course, and meanwhile you had better do as the message said; prepare the third zone of the Aqua World for some alien life forms," said John.

"Very well, and thank you John," I wanted to see what would eventuate from this although it probably amazed John more than myself.

82

I instructed the Marine Supervisor and the Environmental Manager as well as the overseer of the third zone of the Aqua World to prepare for some rare exotic species, I didn't say how rare. The octopi would have to go into the second zone which was ready for the introduction of marine fish.

A week later as I walked along the beach I saw the dolphins out deep in the water, with them was a human swimmer. The dolphins were swimming around this swimmer and sometimes coming so close they could be touched.

I asked the man who feeds the fish if he knew who it was. He said, "That's Mia, Ralf Putney's daughter."

I wondered at her ability to be so friendly with the dolphins and to swim so strongly as she was only about six years of age.

"Wonders happen!" said the fish feeder, "a child with the dolphins, what next."

And I thought, "It is really no wonder, her being my daughter; the daughter of an extra-terrestrial and me being a fish person in the depths of my soul."

83

It was inevitable, several months later an article appeared in an astronomy journal about life in outer space. The article named planet Oberon as a planet where there was life, possibly ocean creatures and perhaps spirit beings which lived in the clouds.

There was no link in the article with myself however in some private quarters apparently my name was being mentioned. I had a phone call from Albert Poute not long after the publication of this article, he said that my perhaps having relations with alien beings may not be the public image that Global Monarch would like for it's management. It may cause panic and a drop in stock values, he advised me not to have anything to do with alien life and to be publicly careful about any divulgences.

I needed some good luck on my side so I decided to see what a woman's persuasion could do. I contacted Kate Poute, and suggested a meeting, she replied that she was unavailable; could we communicate on the internet. So with some help from within the Design Office Department I learnt to make, and made, contact with Kate on the internet.

She said she had been investigating me as she had found herself pregnant. I asked her if she is related to Albert Poute and she said, yes she is. She went on to say that she had fibbed because she didn't want her daughter to be like herself. She had married for money and had only wanted love ever since. She didn't want it to be known that Jennifer was rich, or anything about her family connections. She did not know anything about my message from planet Oberon or links to extra-terrestrials and when I asked her to persuade her father-in-law to let me have a free hand with the third zone of the Holdfast Bay Aqua World she said yes but, could I do something for her.

Kate had seen my statue of Miriam and knew it was very special in it's processes of construction. She asked if I could make one of herself, only smaller, for her garden. I said it would take a lot of planning and involve other people but I would do what I could.

And so it was that I got from her a photograph in the nude, lying, gesturing and pouting. I showed it to Rex and he said, "Oh, another one."

"Yes," said I, "for a friend."

Then I contacted Olivia Octavo and put the proposition to her. "Yes," she said, "but at a price."

"I'll pay," I said.

84

Rex Gonzalez and Olivia Octavo worked on the small statue for the next few months and I was pleased when I went to the laboratory in the basement to view it.

"Friend of yours?" said Martin the laboratory manager.

"Yes, I have many friends but they don't all want a statue for themselves, if that's what you're thinking," I replied.

"Must be a good friend!" said Martin.

"I wanted a favour from her and she wanted this statue, a straight deal," I said, not wanting to reveal anything.

"Nothing to do with aliens is it?" he said.

So the rumours had spread to the Design Office. I was getting talked of, controversially, and I wasn't sure if I liked it.

.   .   .   .

In the next few days as I sat at my desk in the sky room I had two photographs on my desk, one of Miriam and one of Kate, I compared them.

No two humans are exactly alike; I thought; they are similar but always different. Different bodies, different minds. I would say that the two women in the photographs were beautiful but they were both unique and so unalike in nature.

Miriam was more homely and a good mother; Kate was more the type of person who played hard and wanted the pleasures of life, she was even willing to lie, which Miriam never did. I had no doubt which one I preferred. Although they looked similar in the photographs I knew that Miriam was Randy Bilder's archetypical woman, who answered the deepest desires of his sexual and romantic notions of women in general. Miriam, yes she was honest and honesty was very necessary to the bond of marriage, in fact it was essential.

I thought of Miriam, Kate and also Shiree, each one was valuable as a human being in their own ways, each one an individual. The richness of human nature affected me deeply with respect and an awareness that I could not ever know all the natures of all the different humans. It seemed to me that the fish people of planet Oberon were not so finely differentiated. They seemed to have a kind of group or specie mind and as far as I was to know could only mostly communicate on a cerebral, extra-sensory level.

The universe was a strange and wonderful place with space for all varieties of beings; even cloud people, spirit beings. I was not at that time to be aware that the real Randy Bilder was having adventures that would surprise even me, as he explored the full extent of Oberon's many worlds.

85

As I awoke one morning the late autumn sun beamed softly through the curtains. I was aware that Miriam was still asleep and breathing deeply. I sat awake for almost an hour before she stirred and stared at me.

"Randy! It's you, you've come back to me, oh Randy!" and she hugged me tightly.

I was surprised. "No, it's only me, Mr Alien." I said, I didn't want to disappoint her but what could I do.

"Are you sure, I took one look at you this morning and I could have sworn that you were my Randy, my Randy come back to me." Miriam sighed in an exasperated and deflated way.

"Yes," I replied, "I'm still with you. I know you miss your husband but I have a feeling that it won't be much longer. I said I would warn you when I am to go home. It shouldn't be much longer and I'll be gone. Then you will be very pleased, won't you?"

"Oh, yes; I'm disappointed, but if it has to be then I guess I'll just have to accept it," she said.

"Pray tell, what is it about Randy that you miss the most?" said I.

"Well, I don't know. It's just his funny ways. You are just the same physically but he had a better sense of humour, and he was more romantic, not to say more loving," she searched for the words.

I replied. "Well it's hard for me, I'm not used to it; playing the human, but I know I must try harder because I do love you so very much."

On another occasion Miriam was staring at me as we were alone in the lounge room of our house.

"Is anything wrong?" I said.

"It's only that you are very quiet lately and you don't call me angel like Randy used to do," she replied.

"Well perhaps I'm becoming too self absorbed, too absent minded. I worry a lot about what I am meant to be doing here on earth, just what challenges I will have to face. I'm sorry if I seem to ignore you, truly sorry Miriam," I apologised.

"And why don't you ever call me angel," she questioned.

"It never occurred to me. I mean an angel is supposed to be something religious isn't it?" I said.

"Yes but it's romantic to think of me as someone as good and mysterious as an angel, kind of spiritual, and I like being called an angel."

"Yes, I'm sorry I didn't think of it. My! Randy was romantic!" I exclaimed.

"Is romantic, you mean," she said proudly. "I'm sure wherever he is he would be loving someone," she sighed.

"Yes and I must show my love more; angel," I added.

It was about this time, this time in the shorter life of an extra-terrestrial that I began feeling detached from Miriam and also from most other people. I cherished my silent hour being near to the dolphins; to hear their murmurings, their cries of endearment and desire for each other. The sound of their motions, diving and swiftly swimming upwards towards the surface of the waters, and as they touched so closely the sides of the transparent tunnel made me especially attentive to their needs and wants. They were happy creatures with fewer worries than humans and simpler desires.

I felt an almost sexual attraction for them. Not to any one dolphin in particular but just to the subtleties of their general movement and the sounds of bubbles bursting and the waters swirling. It was an erotic attraction and sometimes I found myself with an erection. I left them each time unwillingly, frustrated. I was becoming isolated from other humans whom I felt could not comprehend my frustrated feelings, my emotional plight. There was, alas, little I could do about all this.

. . . .

To ease this feeling of frustration I began swimming at the beach at the Holdfast Bay project. On weekends I went there early in the mornings. I swam for an hour or longer, often under the waters.

I met a little friend there; her name was Mia, my space age baby, Shiree's and my child. She also swam almost every day she said. She loved the water, everything about it. And she especially liked to swim with the dolphins.

Mia was quiet most of the time but I now had a feeling of fellowship, someone who was more like me. It was uncanny that she should have this same love of the waters, the love for the ocean and its creatures. I now felt more happy and contented, and better able to face the many challenges of my daily experiment with being a human.

87

I had been on this planet, in this body, for almost one year. I was frustrated generally and greatly missed my fishy life. But there were diversions: the octopi.

There were many varieties of octopi that had been introduced to the second zone of the Aqua World. There were small, colourful ones that moved quickly in the waves and spread their tentacles back for propulsion as they travelled through the waters of Holdfast Bay. There were varieties of ever increasing size and gradually to be more greyish in colour as they became larger. The largest was very big and moved slowly often in the shallows of the beach or on pontoons that had been provided for them. Mostly they stayed near to the bottom of the basin of the second zone and often near to the observation tunnel. They were the biggest attraction of the Aqua World, along with the dolphins, but now they would have rivals for popularity. Soon the third zone would be completed; the kiosk, the tunnels and soon would arrive from planet Oberon a new collection of especially unusual creatures, alien creatures; would planet earth be ready for them. Would earthlings ever be ready to meet the unknown, the strange and not merely exotic.

88

The gametes from planet Oberon arrived in the first week of my second autumn or rather they appeared. One afternoon they were not present in the completed third zone of the Aqua World, the next morning they were there. Twenty groups of gametes were distributed from the shore to the deep of the basin. Some groupings were floating and all were in shades of yellow; mustard yellow, green yellow or bright yellow, the gametes created a tapestry of colour mixed with patches of sea-weed.

No one knew how they got there, only I suspected that certain spirit beings on Oberon had motivated by some means similar to extra-sensory extension of their powers the relocation of this matter.

It was a grand even momentous occasion, when the life forms of two great planets came into first contact. There were no announcements at first, no celebrations. The authorities were waiting to see the actual mature alien fish before committing themselves.

It would take days or perhaps a week for some specie of alien fish to make their way into human sight as the final though young stage of their existence. The management and supervisors of the Aqua World did not know how to put a value to the new creatures. To most humans who knew of their existence it was beyond comprehension that soon they would be joined by other life forms; suddenly because humans were now close neighbours to each other, the squabbles of races or nations of humans seemed trivial and of no significance compared with this, the coming of a new age.

89

Hoards, crowds and many more people were now camped outside the gates of Holdfast Bay Aqua World waiting to see the merely exotic fish from their own planet. The public had not been informed that they were to witness for the first time, alien creatures.

I was present every day with the staff and some selected journalists. The first we saw of them was some bright yellow starfish with small red tentacles washed up on the beach. No one wanted to get too close but photographs, with zoom-lens cameras, were taken.

The next creature, the most spectacular, was a snake-like dragon, bright green with purple patches raising it's head and tail simultaneously from the surface of the waters. The human onlookers cheered and more video-film of the creature was taken.

From all parts of the third zone, creatures appeared in all shapes and mostly small in size. There were new sightings every moment and as yet none of these creatures had names so a numbering system was devised. There was a list circulating of numbers and descriptions, everyone wanted to see all twenty varieties, but they were not all "hatched."

The journalists compared notes so as to form a uniform report for the morning's papers and the evening television news broadcast. I was as excited as the others; wanting to see what I knew nothing of, the unknown, the unexpected. The whole day we watched and shared these moments of great event on the planet. We were the lucky few, the fortunate.

That night with Miriam at home we watched the news and the first report was concerned that the public should not panic. There was no threat to earthlings from the first appearance in history of actual extra-terrestrial beings on our planet, right here at Holdfast Bay Aqua World.

A second announcement was made by Lord Sotby-Aston. He said that the alien presence in the Southern Hemisphere would not be a threat to English interests there.

We were taken from ourselves with mirth and a feeling of the universe now being one universe where-as before many had thought simply of us and the unknowable. Now we knew!

90

The excitement for me, "Alien X", never ceased. From this day I seemed truly alive and wanted to wander in the tunnels of Aqua World all day, every day. To see the dolphins, the octopi and the coloured dragons.

I was dazed and under the influence of a new and vital force. How was I ever to get back to normal? I had obligations. I could not go on like this day after day, but I did, for weeks. Something, some event greater than this I could not imagine but something would have to bring me out of this dazed wonderment.

.   .   .   .

Then, when I was least expecting it, Miranda my secretary brought me back to reality. I had another message from John Trummer the astronomer at the Space Observatory: *see you as soon as possible.*

The next day I rang the observatory and was told to meet John that afternoon. He greeted me at the door smiling.

"There has been another message from planet Oberon. I don't know how long we can keep up this communication without letting the United Nations Aeronautics Division know about it."

He led me to his office and presented me with a document from Professor Geiger, it read:

Prepare - Pacific Trust Pty. Ltd. - congratulations again RB.

"What does that all mean," smiled John.

"I don't know, I will have to investigate," I replied. "The Pacific, yeh! That somehow seems in order."

"Well I hope you know what you are doing," said John smiling.

"What I don't know I can find out," said I.

.   .   .   .   .

So I returned to the sky office and collected all the information I could about the Pacific. I had the encyclopaedia, books, magazine articles, videos; with tables and graphs and maps. I spread the maps out on the floor and saw the wide, deep extent of the Pacific Ocean. I wondered what I should do and decided to contact my companies to fax me information.

The expanse of the Pacific Ocean was like the sky that I could see from my room. What creatures dwelt in it's depths, what mineral resources did it hold and more to the point, just what was I going to do with such a company as Pacific Trust Pty Ltd. This was a totally new adventure for me, I thought.

91

I was very busy for over a week investigating the Pacific Ocean. I noted specific regions: Northwest Pacific Basin, Central Pacific Basin, Southwest Pacific Basin.

These three regions were each about the size of Australia, but they struck me as being similar to the three zones of the Holdfast Bay Aqua World, only on a much larger scale. Size did not daunt me. Mere colourings on a map or lists of figures didn't affect me. It was a conceptual type of thing. I saw that these three regions could be developed to be similar to the three zones of the Aqua World.

Also I noted deep ocean trenches: Bonin Trench, Miriana Trench, Kermadeck Trench, Tonga Trench.

Surely these were so deep that humans could not go there, so available at a cheap price, I supposed.

And then there were three islands that interested me:- Mariana Island, Tonga Island, Phoenix Island.

These islands were close to the ocean's basins and trenches: they could be developed as bases or bases could be developed on them. I was fascinated, but I then waited for the replies to come in from my companies.

.   .   .   .   .

Within a few days I had all the information I needed, Pacific Extensive Pty. Ltd., and Deep Sea Explorations Worldwide Corporation had faxed me an abundance of various types of data.

It seems that there is a wealth of minerals in the major basins of the Pacific; enough estimated oil to supply the world indefinitely and equally of every other known mineral. It had been just too expensive to mine these resources until now. The basins were considered too inaccessible and just too deep to warrant serious exploration.

I contacted my companies and instructed them to investigate these basins and the trenches, and to seek to buy land on the islands for development as bases for the manufacture of deep ocean edifices.

I next contacted the Tri-Star Company and hired them as a consultant to the other two companies. I said Tri-Star was to contact the two companies with my instructions for the development of transport networks.

After all this I felt it was time to get some advise so I phoned Ralf Putney. He arrived in my office with no expectations but he did have an open mind. He listened to my plans for the Pacific Trust Company and how I was initiating moves for the exploitation of the Pacific Ocean for minerals and fish-farming.

Ralf was amazed, "How did you," he said, "even contemplate such a thing?"

I said that signing with Global Monarch had inspired me but the rest was blind faith. And he replied that I had better keep Global Monarch Incorporated informed of my moves. Otherwise he approved only adding that he wouldn't have had the guts to take on billion dollar deals the way I did. Anyway, he wished me luck.

92

My next move was to contact Albert Poute of Global Monarch Incorporated. I requested a video conference which was arranged for the next week. For the first time I was beginning to feel that I was managing my life and not merely letting other forces, other people manage me. I felt that Randolph Bilder was becoming his own man; I began to feel part of a large league of powers and not just part of a small human team.

I sat in the video conference room and the technician adjusted the microphone and camera. Then I waited and within moments I saw Albert Poute's face on the screen.

"This is Albert Poute, Randolph, how can I help you?"

"It's like this Mr. Poute, I have ambitions for the Pacific Ocean region. I would like a certain development company to become a subsidiary of Global Monarch. This company is to be known as Pacific Trust Pty. Ltd. I have instructed as a member of two company boards to begin plans for the exploitation of the minerals of the Pacific Ocean, the development of fish farming and the investigation of tourist centres. I have hired a local transport company as consultant to these two companies and I would at this stage like your opinion of this display of ambition."

"Well, you make grand moves. Just how do you think it's all going to be feasible and financially viable. I understand the possible benefits of deep ocean mining and your other initiatives but how do you propose to carry this thing through."

"Listen Mr. Poute, you must have faith in me. I have the will to do what has been just an idle dream for hundreds of years and I believe the time is right to go into this. It's time to make bold moves and take advantage of research that has been developing to the stage where, now the Pacific, in fact all the world's oceans can be exploited, and there are huge profits to be made."

"I have been hesitant when I heard about your connection with these extra-terrestrial creatures but I have had a change of heart. Randolph, I'm going to put my faith behind you and trust you on this. There are just a few loose ends we'll have to tie up.

I feel that the venture needs to be tighter in it's organization, financial, and in it's direction; therefore my advice is to go ahead with any purchases of property, I know ocean deeps are cheap on the market, no use to anyone, so go ahead by all means but I would like you to make this local transport company you are dealing with into a subsidiary of Global Monarch, and bring the three companies together under the direction of one company with a board of management taken from the managing directors of the separate companies; and you Randolph direct the lot as managing director of this company; Pacific Trust Pty. Ltd. . How does that sound to you, Randolph."

"Excellent Mr. Poute, I shall certainly take your advice and I am glad to have your full support of my initiatives. Thank you very much, Mr. Poute."

"Thanks for consulting me, Randolph, thanks from me and my family. Goodbye."

93

It was only a week later and I had in my hands a trans-script of my conversation with Albert Poute; letters containing the proposals to the three companies, signed by Albert Poute himself and a notification to finalize the legal proceedings for the inauguration of Pacific Trust Pty. Ltd. I was to contact a certain lawyer, Stanley Poute of Brookland to sign the documents.

I contacted Stanley Poute the same day as I received the letters from Global Monarch. Stanley replied promptly, I was to be in Brookland the following day. I took an early morning flight and arrived in Brookland by mid-morning. I signed the documents in the presence of Stanley who was now more congenial than he had been the last occasion that we had met.

We had lunch together at which time he informed me that he would personally arrange the inauguration party. I didn't know what he meant and he explained that such an important event as the formation of a new Global Monarch company would have to be celebrated in a big way. We would have to show to other dignitaries and important persons that Global Monarch supported the new company, this meaning that future support for the company was formally requested. I agreed with this formality and he said the party would be in about one month's time in Brookland. Events of this nature and stature usually were held in Green Court House. Many state functions were held there, said Stanley, and this was the place to celebrate the status of the occasion in a fitting setting.

I agreed again and soon after we parted wishing each other the best for the future. I caught the afternoon flight back and arrived home in time for dinner.

All was well; I Alien X had faith that on the other side of the universe plans were also being made; the real Randolph Bilder would perhaps be organizing some magnificent celebration, the fish people would be aware that there were new forces in the universe, and the spirit beings, the cloud people of Oberon would be ever omni-present, in some way smiling on us all.

94

It was now a time for returning to the past, a past which I, Alien X, cherished for its wealth of memories. It had been many years since I had first visited planet earth. I had stayed many months and then returned to planet Oberon. This second time I had stayed a full year; I had experienced a spring and summer my first time here; an autumn and winter the second time, now another spring was with us.

Miriam reminded me, we were going to Stockport, to the mountains, to the snow. Every year Miriam and Randy, Spin and Siri went on holidays to Stockport. This year was to be no different except Pamela would be accompanying Spin. For me, Alien X it would be the first time that we would all be going, although I, as Randolph, had been on holiday with the family and Pamela several times.

Pamela was the mayor's daughter and the mayor and I were friends and associates in this city of new and exciting attractions. Pamela knew me as Spin's father, her father's business friend and, as an assistant manager at the Tri-Star company, she knew me quite well then; as someone whom she respected and admired and also to some extent credit was due to me for the elevation of Tri-Star from a local transportation company to a big player in Global Monarch's stable of subsidiaries.

When Miriam, I and Siri set out in the family car, Spin and Pamela followed in their car. Although Siri had had lessons to drive a car she did not as yet have her own car. I was driving and remembering being a passenger over six years before, going to Stockport; and I remembered that trip. The thought of skiing again, was on my mind, as we sped along the auto-way. Siri may have forgotten my ineptness and my show of silly ignorance at not knowing what snow was, but I was remembering.

After several hours of driving I got into the passenger seat and Miriam drove, just as it had been all that long time ago. It was refreshing to get away from work and experience this freedom and these memories. It was also very refreshing to again feel the breeze lifting my hair as it blew passed.

We were soon at Stockport and as we rounded the cliffs I saw the small town once again in the valley. The mountains seemed higher than they were years before and the snow whiter. We slowed down and drove into the chalet car park and then there we were once more snug and warm inside. I looked around sentimentally remembering the wood panelling in the large lounge and the open wood-fire in its place.

A great contentment swept over me as I realized the joy of re-experiencing something that had been so new and earthly the first time around. I slept very well that night and all of us went skiing in the morning. Again, that feeling of joy as I skied, experiencing and re-experiencing at the same time.

We were all quite good except Pamela who many times fell on the snow and had to abandon her attempts at skiing. We went in to the chalet exhausted and had a fine lunch.

The drive home was as the first time; we all had great appetites and ate heartily at the restaurants along the way. It was a very enjoyable week with the family and I hoped then, that I would still be on earth to experience the snow next September holidays.

95

I now played a waiting game. Certain circumstances had to be in order, a certain configuration of events before I could progress any further.

I visited the Aqua World about once a week and was amazed at how fast the dragons grew. They were already twice the size of what they were when they made their first appearance. I sat many hours during the long days in my sky office. I did Miriam's clueless cross-word puzzles and logic problems.

Some correspondence came from Stanley Poute who was now Pacific Trust's legal advisor. The two subsidiaries of Global Monarch had agreed to the new organizational structure and Tri-Star Corporation had been absorbed into Global Monarch's empire.

I received reports from these companies about research and investigations. Properties had been bought on the three islands in the Pacific and plans had been put into operation for the building of bases for the Pacific development project.

Miriam and I still went on our evening walks which were very enjoyable in the pleasant spring air and light. I also continued to go to the gym once a week and because of this I was feeling very fit.

Life at that moment could not be better.

96

Miriam and I set out for the airport on the day of the inauguration party. Siri was to go with Spin and Pamela. I, of course having no experience of such a formal celebration was apprehensive. I was to dress in a special suit Miriam and I had bought the week before and wear a bowtie. I was wearing a normal suit but was to change into formal wear at a hotel in central Brookland. Miriam looked quite stunning in a black gown.

When we arrived at Green Court House I was quite astonished. Here were large gates with Olivia Octavo's faces staring out at me. And, as we entered the driveway in our hired limousine there were large flaming lamps every five metres that Miriam said were flambeau lighting.

As we took the first step up to the entrance of Green Court House, Miriam reached out her hand and stopped me, "You look just like a movie star," she said smiling like an angel.

"I didn't know I was handsome," said I.

"Ruggedly handsome," she replied as she squeezed my hand.

97

We entered the lobby of Green Court House and were greeted by four people, the Mayor of my home town and his wife, the Mayor of Brookland and her husband. They welcomed us, shaking hands and directed us into a large reception hall.

Here were hundreds of people most of whom I had never seen before. As we walked around I was approached by couples and individuals who wished us well. There was Rex Gonzales and his wife, Boz Brennon the Landscape Architect Departments young assistant, Olivia Octavo , and Ralf Putney with a vivacious looking Shiree. There was Stanley Poute, and his wife Kate looking mischievous, Spin and Pamela looking bright and excited, and Siri scanning the crowd for eligible young men.

We were introduced to countless people, all very important dignitaries of Brookland. It was several hours of talking and smiling and exchanging good wishes. Everyone wanted to know Miriam and I. Everyone wanted to congratulate me and meet Miriam for they had all seen her statue.

We helped ourselves to a large assortment of foods displayed on a large side table and waiters waltzed through the crowd with trays of champagne. I was not used to this exciting drink and was feeling quite merry.

Then as I was beginning to get a little weary with it all I saw Stanley Poute get up onto a stage at the end of the hall. He adjusted a microphone and began:

Good evening Ladies and Gentlemen. My name is Stanley Poute, representing Global Monarch Incorporated. I have the pleasure tonight of announcing the formation of a new company, Pacific Trust Pty. Ltd. The Managing Director of this new company is Mr. Randolph Bilder, currently Manager of the City Design Office in the city where he resides.
Pacific Trust Pty. Ltd. is a major subsidiary company of Global Monarch Incorporated. Not only this, but Pacific Trust Pty. Ltd. will be overseeing three lesser companies, all subsidiaries of Global Monarch Incorporated.

Mr. Randolph Bilder has the full support and backing of his endeavours with Pacific Trust Pty. Ltd. in the development of the Pacific region. I, as representative of Global Monarch Incorporated, hope that everyone here tonight will fully support and encourage Randolph Bilder now and in the future. Please join with me in this momentous event and celebrate heartily. Thank you Ladies and Gentlemen.

Next to mount the stage was the Mayor of my home city:

Welcome ladies and gentlemen to this truly wondrous occasion. I am the Mayor of Randolph Bilder's city of origin which thanks to him we are calling The City of Wonders. We are a fortunate city for Randolph Bilder has made it so.
On this occasion, the formation of a new company named Pacific Trust Pty. Ltd. Randolph's home town is going to celebrate. As Randolph Bilder has brought credit and renown to this city so too will he bring credit and renown to his new company. We join you all here tonight in celebrating the creation of this company, Pacific Trust Pty. Ltd. and I on behalf of Randolph's home city, the City of Wonders, thank him for his past creations and what we believe will be a brilliant future for his company.

The Mayor of Brookland was next to give a speech, she quickly said her piece:

As Mayor of the city of Brookland I know that Randolph Bilder has done great things for his home city. I also know that Randolph Bilder will again do great things with Pacific Trust Pty. Ltd.

Although Brookland is a regional centre it has powers and influence far beyond it's geographical extent. This power and influence I as Mayor of Brookland promise will be in full support of Pacific Trust Pty. Ltd. . Anything that the citizens of Brookland can do to assist Randolph Bilder I hereby pledge they shall do and I sincerely wish this endeavour great success.

Thank you Randolph for what you have done for this region in the past and best wishes for the future.

Finally Ralf Putney got up onto the stage and gave a short speech.

As a friend and business associate of Randolph Bilder I ask you to join with me in giving three hearty cheers for Randolph and Pacific Trust Pty. Ltd. .

Cheers went up from the crowd. Then as I was aware that it was my duty and I had prepared a speech the day before, I stepped up onto the stage and adjusted the microphone to my greater height. I announced.

I am Randolph Bilder. It is with great gratitude and honour that I accept these wishes of good fortune for the future. I find I must thank all of my business associates especially Rex Gonzalez for his help and inspiration over the years.

I must also thank Global Monarch Incorporated for this wonderful opportunity. And also thanks unendingly to my wife Miriam Bilder without whom I could not have achieved what I have done. Thank you everyone.

As I stepped down from the stage the crowd cheered and Miriam flooded into my arms. Then we almost all went into another hall where a small orchestra was playing slow songs and many people began to dance. As I was not to keen on the idea of dancing and knew little about it we decided to get it over with as soon as possible. Miriam led me to the centre of the dance hall and breathing heavily I clung to her as she steered me about. It was like a dream, the music, the crowd of faces and Miriam so close to me. Then a spotlight settled on Miriam and I and the crowd drew back. We danced to some slow romantic tune as everyone watched and seemingly held their collective breath, for it was such a romantic scene.

Not long after the dance I was scanning the crowd for familiar faces when I saw Shiree and Kate. They were standing close together, laughing and seemingly sharing some secret. Then when they saw me looking their way they both turned away and held their hands behind their backs. Both Shiree and Kate holding one finger in the other hand looked back over their shoulders and then turned again smiling. I was a little embarrassed but guessed that they had been talking about me and was not too worried that these women had a secret that the general public would die to know.

Late that night we exited the large doors of Green Court House and entered our limousine. Cameras flashed and we were sure we would be seen on tomorrow's TV. news. Miriam said, "Well, that's over."

"Yes," I said, "the celebration is over."

98

The following day I felt a little of an after-climax. I was still in a state of excitement, flitting about the house in an exuberant mood. I was also slightly under the weather from drinking the champagne.

I said to Siri, "And did you meet any exciting young men, Boz Brennon for example."

"Oh yes, hundreds, and Boz of course, but one especially took my fancy; Casel Poute," she replied gaily.

Casel Poute "Casel Poute," said I, "Do you mean the son of Stanley Poute and the brother of Jennifer Poute."

"The very same; I was very impressed, Casel is very sweet," Siri hummed.

"Well wonders never cease," I said, "I had no idea that Stanley Poute had a son."

"Well he has," said Siri, "and I'm meeting him tomorrow, we're going to the Aqua World together."

"Oh! Well, er, have fun and say hello to the dragons for me," I intoned my approval.

. . . . .

The ways of humans always amazed me; the way we meet new people, become friendly and sometimes bond more securely, clinging like pieces of driftwood in the back-waters of this part of the planet.

Siri and Casel became an item for the newspapers over the next few months. They were often together at night clubs here and in Brookland, at the beach and at various places were young couples were wont to frequent.

I gradually became accustomed to his face in the house and he seemed a charming young man. He was I assumed similar to Jennifer Poute in many ways, and he insisted that when he was in Paris he was known as *Casel Poute*, with an accent.

99

A week went by and I was still to come down from my high feeling of exuberance after the inauguration party. Of course I had high hopes for Pacific Trust Pty. Ltd. but how could I possibly live up to the well wishes of all those people who encouraged me and inspired me to make of this new company the success it deserved to be.

I couldn't concentrate on any one thing for very long and tended to spend much time with Miriam just chatting and drinking lots of coffee and cokes.

Then in my office one bright inspiring morning, Miranda, my secretary entered.

"You have a message from a Mr. John Trummer at the observatory. He said to call there personally anytime," Miranda informed me.

So, a feeling of apprehension immediately overtaking me, I drove quickly out to the observatory.

"Hello," said John Trummer, "and how are you this fine day."

"Fine thanks," I said, "do you have something to talk to me about."

"Yes," he paused, "we astronomers at the observatory have been having discussions with the United Nations Aeronautics and Space Division;" he paused again. "They haven't any more information about planet Oberon but they say that the extra-terrestrial creatures, the alien fish could not have come all this distance from Oberon by normal space ships or other craft. They say the creatures must have arrived here by some process of the telepathic transmigration of matter." He stopped abruptly then continued, "There is no space vehicle or craft, the creatures just appeared overnight therefore they say it must be *this,* and they link it with these Spirit Beings, the Cloud People of planet Oberon." He was silent then.

"Well I suppose anything is possible when dealing with extra-terrestrial forces. I suppose we will just have to wait and see what develops. I certainly can throw no light on the matter, I'm just as puzzled as you are."

I ruminated a little for his benefit, then I left him and returned to my office feeling a strange excitement and a premonitory desire to speed time; to see what would eventuate from this unusual conclusion of the United Nations Aeronautics and Space Division.

100

It seemed that I just had to drift for awhile. My blind faith in developing Pacific Trust Pty. Ltd. had reached an impasse. I felt that the three subsidiaries under my watchful eye could continue as though part of some automatic process, some force greater than myself. I learnt that often in business the organisation took care of itself and generated forces entirely of it's own, forces that would lead to new horizons, new challenges and it was not for me to interfere but merely to caste my benevolent eye occasionally at a map or report and then relax. Yes, just relax, life was good; all was well with the world and I felt, with the entire universe.

.   .   .   .

My evening walks with Miriam were a delight. We were having exceptionally fine days for that time of year. The usual storms and strong winds that coloured springtime with the marks of change did not happen. The days were calm, the air warm and still as the sun shone through great tufts of clouds and the sunsets were especially spectacular.

This evening in particular, I had a feeling of relaxed calm, of well being as I strolled with Miriam and we exchanged stories. We; I especially, wondered at the cows and sheep we saw through the hedges at the sides of country lanes. But I was not excited by these land-bound earthling creatures. They were fine for eating the meat of but just to see them idly browsing the grasses, so unaffected by the twilight haze that settled over the countryside; no I was less than excited by these lesser animals.

Then I looked up as we walked back the way we had come and as we neared our street I noticed *that* star in the night sky. The star of yellow, the star called Oberon. At first it just caught my wandering eyes, then as I looked more closely it became more distinct, more separate in that vast array of lights.

I stopped Miriam and pointed Oberon out to her, but she only saw patches of stars and occasionally a star more bright, but not one yellow, not one more distinct from others.

As I looked I was drawn in upon it, my consciousness, my awareness focussing; becoming unaware of any other sight or sound. I stared transfixed and as the first time my consciousness telescoped in upon itself and I could receive at first vague vibrations which then I perceived as the bursting of bubbles, their sound pulsating and communicating in the language of the fish people of Oberon.

I stood dazed and Miriam watched me - awestruck. I concentrated harder to receive the message that travelled through space from Oberon to Earth where I, Alien X could be the only one who would receive it. It was my sign, my signal, I was soon to depart home, home to Oberon on the other side of the universe.

I immediately shook my awareness back to reality, the reality of Miriam and the warm spring evening.

"I've had my message," I said, "I am soon to go back where I came from."

"Randy will be back," exclaimed Miriam excitedly, and then, "and you will be gone. First Randy then you, then Randy then you again; you come and go and I stay and wait, and I forget what it's like to be without either of you. I think it's very strange and it's sad that you two come and go. But it must be a thousand times stranger for you both." She was quiet then.

I was quiet, then I said, "We fish people and humans must learn each other's ways for I have a feeling that we are going to live more closely, know each other more intimately and we will learn to respect each other and live in harmony."

It was only a feeling, but I felt that my time on earth was not for nothing; destiny was bound to bring the two peoples together for I believed we had much in common, much to share and in the matrix of time that had hitherto separated us soon we would know that this is one universe where a common dream would bind us in a united future.

Did the real Randolph Bilder think this way I wondered, did he have secret hopes that no-one as yet knew, did he have anyone to share his hopes with; or was he having some strange encounter with the spirit beings of Oberon. Following my feelings of certainty about the common destiny of the two peoples, fish and human, I had doubts, about these spirit beings and their powers and I feared that Randolph may be in an even stranger situation than myself. If only I knew what was happening to the real Randolph Bilder.

As I walked along the beach of Holdfast Bay this morning to pay my last respects, I watched the birds and the waves and the birds as they swooped down from the skies and skimmed the surface of the water.

I looked further passed the waves and there was Mia, my space child, and she was riding on the back of a dolphin. "Hello Mia," I laughed out loud and there was no-one to hear me. I heard her voice calling to me and she waved, then the dolphin came in close to the shore. Mia dove off into the waters and swam the last few metres until she could stride with the waves.

"Hello," I said, "and how are you today?"

"Very well," she gasped breathlessly. "My dolphins take me all over the bay, but I know they aren't the spirit beings. The spirit beings will come later."

"What was that?" I was surprised. "How do you know that?" I quizzed her.

"I have feelings, I understand things that others don't know about. I just know the spirit beings will come!" she said assertively.

"Oh! Well Mia, if you say so then it must be true," I didn't want to upset her and how was I to know that what she was saying wasn't true. She apparently had had some communication with the sky people of Oberon.

I took her little hand and we walked along the beach. Soon we came upon the person of the Manager of Aqua World.

"Good morning," he smiled at us.

"Good day," we both said at the same time.

"You know," he said, "Mia is so good with the dolphins, we've been watching her every day. The way she can ride on their backs is amazing, we might just hire her as an added attraction of the Aqua World."

"Yes, please do!" exclaimed Mia.

"Well, we're seriously thinking of it so don't be surprised if we make you an offer one day soon," he kept smiling.

I knew him well by now so I could tell that he was sincere and was really serious about having Mia as a paid attraction.

"There aren't many like you, Mia," he laughed.

And then Mia and I continued our walk along the beach until I had to say a sad goodbye. Little did Mia know but I am her real father and in a few short days I would be replaced by the real Randolph Bilder who knew nothing of her but may notice her one morning if he came to this beach and searched out deep where the dolphins frolic.

102

That afternoon, after my conversation with Mia, I sat in my sky office. How much longer it would be mine I was not to know, but definitely not much longer. Then it would be Randolph's again, funny that. I come, he goes; I go, he comes and then it starts all over again, trading places from one end of the universe to the other. Space travellers on some extra-sensory wave-length seemingly never aligned, never bound to be in the same place at the same time. An odd way to be but that's destiny and fish people as well as humans were seeming victims of destiny, not knowing what the future would bring next. But what of the spirit beings of Oberon, did these cloud people live above destiny, did they in fact control the destinies of lesser beings; I wondered if this might be so and if so why?

Late in the afternoon Miranda, my secretary, entered my office. "Urgent video conference with Albert Poute, immediately," she declared.

.   .   .   .

I plugged myself into the video conference equipment and was directly confronted with the imposing image of Albert on the video screen.

"Are you receiving me, Randolph," he sighed deeply.

"Yes, very clearly," I said, "and can you see me."

"Yes, Randolph, clear vision, clear sound," he paused thoughtfully.

"There are several things I am wanting to inform you of. Firstly, Global Monarch is backing you one hundred percent in this Pacific deal. I tried to buy the three basins that you were wanting but the United Nation's ordinances forbid it. The best I could do was to get indefinite leases. So they are yours to do what you want with," he paused again with an air of great importance.

"Also besides the land you wanted for the bases on those islands we have purchased several smaller islands that will be available for any use that you want to make of them, airports for example. And, not only this, but we were able to purchase the ocean trenches at a rock bottom price. No-one wants them, they are so deep no-one can get down to them. So I hope that you are pleased that we now have these properties under the belt of Global Monarch and at your disposal." He paused again to let me deliberate.

"Well that's the first announcement, the second is that I have been hearing reports from a relative of mine, Casel Poute my grandson, that he is getting in a very serious relationship with your daughter Siriona. Do you know anything about that?"

"Well I have been seeing a lot of Casel at my house," I replied eagerly to his question, "he is a very fine young man and yes I do believe that Siriona; we call her Siri, is very taken with him as well, so we will have to wait and see what develops."

"Very well, I wish them luck and also I wish the very best to Pacific Trust Pty. Ltd. and yourself." He seemed to be waiting for me to reply but I couldn't think what to say right at that moment.

"Well, I'll be going now - goodbye Randolph," he said.

"Goodbye Mr. Poute and thank you for your faith and good wishes," said I.

The video screen went blank as I sat blinking at the receding glow of Albert's image.

Although I was extremely glad to have the best wishes of Albert Poute and to have these assets now available to me, I also felt that it was now all up to Randolph Bilder not me, Alien X, who would be gone again into the sky, to Oberon from whence I came.

Randolph would have to take up the reigns and guide this plan to it's destination. How much the spirit beings of Oberon had to do with it I wasn't at that time to ascertain; maybe Randolph knew more than I did. So it was now for him to carry on, like a team-mate in some cosmic relay race; when morning's destiny awoke him and brought him back to his Earth, his home.

103

"Ahrr, mmm; Good morning Randy," Miriam turned in their bed to him.

"Ahrr, yes, Miriam," Randy blinked into the still dim light. "Good morning, Miriam," he paused blankly. "It's me again, your old Randy, I've returned from my adventures."

"Oh! Yes!" cried Miriam excitedly. "He told me you would return to me any morning now, so how are you?"

"Oh very well, still in one piece; still alive and kicking," Randy kicked up his legs and waved his arms, examined his hands and touched his face, "Yes, it's me, and have I got a story for you this time."

"I don't know, have you?" questioned Miriam eagerly awaiting to hear some strange tale from the distant reaches of the universe.

It was all a bit much for them both and they decided to talk about it at a later time, but for now Randy put his arm around Miriam's shoulder and drew her into a long kiss that was hard and soft and greeting her with all the longing that seemed suddenly to be swelling his soul and heating his body.

She knew, Miriam knew; time apart was time lost and though Mr. Alien would bring fond memories it was Randy her real husband who was now with her, wanting her and she breathed a long sigh of sheer joy.

PART 3

Alien X and the Great Colonization

I returned to earth and to the body of Randolph Bilder with a feeling of some trepidation. Great things were expected of me but I was not to know until my actual arrival what Randy had achieved during my five earth years away. The Pacific Ocean was opening to colonization by my fish-people from the planet of Oberon and I was in some way expected to direct this settlement.

Many unexpected challenges would I have to face, and the sense of fulfilment as I was finally to see my people emerge from the deep ocean and take their place amongst earthly creatures and humans was the greatest thrill for any alien; fish-person, or human.

Alien X
Winter 2035

104

A multitude of colours and shapes swirled before my closed eyes. I heard the chirping of birds as in some primeval dream time before I became aware of the dimensions of my body. I could feel the weight of my body, then the beating of my heart; then as I stretched, my limbs, my toes and fingers coming to life, awakening.

I breathed deep the fine sweet air of planet earth. Light flooded into my consciousness as I opened my eyes. It was too bright in the filtered light of the bedroom. I closed my eyes. I lay in a thoughtless swirling joy of chaotic imagery. The colours swirled in curling shafts as points of light hit my closed eyelids. My body was like a womb in which I dwelt independent of the outside world. I began to think, I am; I am Randolph Bilder. I am the husband of Miriam Bilder. This far I could go; I had memory. I knew that I had an earth family, that I had important work to do here on earth and yes I thought, I am alone of my people. I am the lonely alien; Alien X.

105

"Hi-ho!" I said cheerily. I knew Miriam would not be exactly happy about my return to her husband's body but I wanted the re-introduction to be as smooth and painless as possible.

"Mmmm–Mmmm" moaned Miriam. Then a cheerful, "Good morning, Randy."

"Good morning Miriam," I replied.

"Good but very cold," she said, and suddenly I realized that it was cold outside the bed and the windows were frosty.

It must be winter I thought. "Yes well at least it's nice and warm in bed." I said.

"Yes but this winter seems to go on forever, always dull grey skies and lots of rain."

"Well," I eased it in, "maybe I can take your mind off the weather."

"Yes, how?" she replied.

"I have to inform you once again that...." She interjected, "you're taking us away for a weekend."

"Not exactly, but I have to take you away from your husband for a short while," said I.

"Oh no! Is it true, is it you, is it Mr. Alien returned to Earth?"

She sat up in bed and looked searchingly into my eyes. "Yes....it's you again, but it's been a *long* time and I don't know about Randy going again," she paused. "But yes, I'm sad....and happy too. You see, I did miss you."

"Oh yes Miriam, and I realize now how much I miss you. The sound of your voice, the smiling face, would make any earthman pine away with loneliness if he had to be away from you for any great length of time. And me having been far away on planet Oberon seems to make it more intense now that I see you again," my feelings swelled at the sight of her long flowing blond hair.

"You haven't changed a bit," I said.

"Oh! A little older, a little wiser," Miriam replied.

"I know that people change over time," I said, "but I hope you haven't changed too much. Still the same trusting, cheerful soul you always were."

"I hope so, I mean I believe so," She said breathing deeply, more relaxed, now.

We embraced and before we knew it we were both asleep again. It just happens that way sometimes, even when the husband is the well known, Alien X.

106

I had the week-end before I was to go back to work at the Design Office. Miriam was moody most of the time but often she overflowed with emotion and information about what the real Randy Bilder had been doing.

Miriam told me about Randy's activities on earth, and on planet Oberon. On earth Randy had worked unceasingly to prepare for the settlement of fish-people and an eco-world of their needs in the Pacific Ocean. He had made good use of Pacific Trust Pty. Ltd. in developing the three basins of the Pacific, as well as mining facilities on the three islands in the three basins, for processing and shipping, he had developed the three uninhabited islands in close proximity to them. He had directed research into the fishing and farming of these regions and constructed airports, various shelters and mating cubicles.

Randy had just finished the planning for tourist Aqua Worlds on the main islands with special areas for displaying marine creatures from Oberon when he had received a message through John Trummer at the space observatory; the fish-people, their gametes, were to arrive the next month. He had been expecting this and had had particular zones set aside and provisions made for their presence.

He had flown on a tour of facilities in the Pacific; South, Central, and North basins and was present when the gametes appeared in a yellow foam floating on the calm bays of the islands. He arranged as at Holdfast Bay Aqua World for supplementary food to be supplied and found that many small fishes and sea plants from Oberon were useful for this purpose. As well as sub-species from Oberon for the fish-people to farm they were to be responsible for farming many varieties of earth fishes.

In time it was expected that the fish-people could operate mining operations in the deeper zones of the three basins. I was quite amazed at this news and at the facility of Randy Bilder. I was to be even more amazed by what Miriam told me of Randy's adventures on planet Oberon.

107

Oberon we knew was a planet in a solar-system far from earth. The fish-people were the highest life form on the ground although they spent most of their lives in the oceans. The startling thing about Oberon was the presence of the Spirit Beings; the cloud people.

Apparently they had not originated on Oberon but had transported themselves to Oberon many hundreds of thousands of years earlier than this time. They were psychic creatures who existed on vibratory levels of consciousness in the clouded atmosphere of Oberon. They did not possess bodies as such, but were pure fields or centres of psychic energy that communicated at various strata of age. It was assumed that they could not die and at some levels they collectively had endured for the full period of their presence on Oberon.

Most fish-people however were not aware of the psychic capability of the Spirit Beings. It was only in relatively recent times when the fish-people began to consume a certain marine plant that their consciousness had gained the potential of sub-conscious functioning. The peaceful co-existence of fish-people and Spirit Beings had been enhanced by the use of this plant which had the ability of deepening the conscious memory and telepathic abilities of the fish people. There was now some directed evolution of the fish-people, they had started to organize themselves and to go about their lives in a more constructive and fruitful way. They were able now to protect themselves from other marine predators by utilizing substances they obtained from their marine environment to deter them. They were more efficient at fish and plant farming and protected themselves so well that they had extended their lives by an extra ten Oberon years. In many ways life had improved for the fish-people in recent times.

One aspect of this felicitous interaction was the blossoming of an art form that was a product of the Spirit Beings' benevolence. This was the ability of the fish-people to conjure psychic imagery in the air above the waters of Oberon. They constructed, in groups, apparitions that lasted from a few weeks to several months. These apparitions were apparently very colourful and phenomena of great beauty and value to the lives of the fish-people.

Being an extra-terrestrial fish-person I had no memory of these wondrous things that I had known so plainly on my own planet. These things were all revealed to me during my weekend with Miriam; I had the essence of being but was not as yet manifesting my true nature.

108

It was a surprise to me to learn that Spin and Pamela had relocated to the Pacific region, they now lived and worked on Tonga Island in the South Pacific basin. Pamela, being a regional manager of the Global Monarch subsidiary, Tri Star, was responsible for developing models of transportation networks there which would be duplicated in the other two regional basins. They also had had a son, Randy's grandson named Rubin.

More surprising was that Siri had married Casel Poute and they now also lived in the Pacific Ocean region. They had their home and Casel's legal business with Global Monarch in the Central Pacific basin on the island of Mariana.

Having been informed of these events I was feeling as though I had missed a great slice of life during my absence. But life goes on, the planets spin, and lives change and move forward in the dance of existence that cannot for a moment be held back, and looked at without a feeling suggestive of a lack of subjective determination. Each from our own point of view see life unfold as we continue on our separate paths on that never ending journey called destiny.

109

I had learnt much about human vanity during my visits to Earth. Humans liked to glorify themselves or have heroes to glorify. Yes it is true and this I felt was different from my feelings about fish-people who treated each other more or less the same and shared equally in any glory due to individuals.

In my first week of return to the City Design Office I received a message from the city board. A disused gorge was to be developed as a linier park and I was to be responsible for dressing it up and making it a suitable edification to the glory of the city.

With this in mind I visited Rymel Gorge on the southern inner city side and found an overgrown, wild area with a creek flowing through it. I could imagine this gorge having lawns and trees and shrubs with rises and falls in the elevation. I could also see that the creek could be dammed and controlled and formed into ponds and small waterfalls.

Then with the glorification of the city in mind I felt it would be a very good idea to erect statues of prominent citizens of the past, people who had made a contribution to the city's history. I also believed that these statues could be constructed of the boron/mercury material giving the park and the city an original attraction all of its own.

Later that week I met Ralf for a game of golf one afternoon and discussed the linier-park with him. He was more than pleased with the idea of the statues and promised to obtain twenty photographs of formerly prominent citizens.

During the next month I visited the site of the linear-park almost every day and had meetings with the surveyor and hydrologist. I enjoyed doing sketches of how I believed the park should look when completed, and passed these and my advice from consultants on to Rex Gonzalez in the Landscape Architects office where most of the design work would take place.

This work kept me more than occupied and I found I had no time to think about fish-people or the Pacific region. My time would come, I presumed.

110

The days became warmer and the birds sounded nearer and louder and sweeter. The warmth of the sun penetrated my skin even as I took those long evening walks with Miriam into the countryside.

It was an odd feeling now that Spin and Siri were gone from our family home. And yet, it was a feeling I enjoyed, the intimacy with Miriam; speaking now more openly and allowing for little gems of endearment.

It was springtime, time for our yearly holiday week at Stockhaven. It was different without the rest of the family. There was more peace, more tranquillity, we travelled alone and our sharing of silence was like a great calm reward for years of sacrificing ourselves to the family.

We turned round the mountain road and there again was Stockhaven surrounded by snow capped peaks. We settled into our room with the big four-poster bed and had to merge in the peace of each other as soon as we were truly alone. Night and morning we merged and swam in a sea of tranquil togetherness. We never had felt closer to each other.

We went up on the ski-lift every morning and several times skied down the steep slopes. It was a true feeling of freedom and an awareness of the danger as we tried ever more difficult paths down to the chalet and our night-time reveries.

The food was great, the wood fire blazed; it was cool in the mountains but we were strong and healthy and only too willing to rest from the day's excitement in the privacy of our own seclusion. These joys I can never and will never forget.

111

Most of my time now for several months was taken up with the Rymel Linear Park development. Rex Gonzalez and Boz Brennon were doing all the statues and I was spending a lot of time co-ordinating contractors as well as other City departments. I did want some other feature besides the statues but as yet I could not think of anything suitable.

I kept an hour or so a day to spare for checking on Pacific Trust Pty. Ltd. and it's composite companies. The tourist parks were developing quite rapidly however it was taking longer to accustom the fish-people to their tasks of fish farming and mining. The facilities required were extensive and needed rather a long time to establish the bases on the ocean floors. There were however no problems with the fish-people actually living in the three basin zones although seasonal acclimatization meant a reorientation of their individual sensibilities. Apparently they were liking their new home and soon there would be thousands of them working, playing and perhaps constructing apparitions in the skies above the Pacific.

112

Approximately three months into my third visit to planet Earth I received an urgent e-mail from Casel Poute on Phoenix Island, Central Pacific. He wanted me to do something about a problem that was creating concern among the workers in each of the three basin zones.

It appeared that fourteen workers divided between the three zones had gone missing. At this early stage he was unable to say what had happened to them. However he suspected foul play on behalf of the fish-people because each person missing had been working in the ocean near fish-people.

I did not know what to think. Casel went on to say that he would have to inform his grandfather, Albert Poute.

This was on my mind over the next few days and I was very concerned about the missing men and the implications involving the fish-people.

113

It was almost a week after Casel's email had arrived. I had done nothing but worry. Late in the afternoon Miranda, my secretary entered my office and told me that there was an urgent video conference arranged immediately with Albert Poute.

I entered the video conference room in a very uneasy state of mind. I sat in front of a video screen and the image of Albert Poute came onto the screen.

"Are you receiving my image Randolph," said Albert.

"Yes, very well thank you," I said.

"Well this affair of the missing workers is causing us great concern. We must solve this problem immediately. I want you to fly out to the Central Pacific zone, Phoenix Island and get to the bottom of this problem. If anyone can do it, you can. So far we are regarding the mystery of the missing workers as an industrial safety issue, that's what we tell the press and that's what you will tell anyone who enquires about it.

I have arranged the trip on the space shuttle. The confirmation ticket will be faxed to you as soon as possible and we want this matter cleared up in a week or two so that things can get back to normal."

"OK, Randolph?" He said.

"Yes," I replied, "I will leave immediately and I'll do my very best to solve this problem, thank you."

114

I directly informed the Board through Ralf Putney that I would be taking two weeks research leave.

That night I told Miriam that I would be going. She was upset at first but when I explained the reason she understood the importance and urgency of the trip.

The next morning I received the faxed tickets for the next day. I had to fly to Brookland and then to an airport nearby that only launched space craft. Miriam had my bags packed by the time I got home from work and I settled down to a restless night's sleep before my first flight on a space shuttle.

115

I travelled to Brookland on the early flight and then by taxi to the space airport.

A rocket and it looked very much like the kind of rocket I had seen on TV, used to launch satellites, was on a launch pad and I had to go up an elevator to a small plane that was attached to it's outside. I entered and found a small cabin containing five seats in which sat men dressed in casual comfortable looking clothes.

These men, I was to learn were various types of engineers that were to work with Global Monarch in the Pacific.

The rocket took off with a jarring speed that pressed my body back against the seat and head rest. The rocket levelled out after a few minutes and we travelled in silent flight, except for music over head-phones, for several hours. The small plane detached itself at that stage and descended quickly to the ground where we landed conventionally at Phoenix airport.

It had taken as long to get to Phoenix Island as it had taken to fly from my home city to Brookland and I felt fresh and ready to meet the fish people from Oberon.

116

As I descended from the small shuttle plane I was aware of a roaring high pitched wavering drone that was rich with harmony and sounded pleasant to my ears. I was totally mystified as to what the sound could be.

On the ground I was met by Casel Poute and Siri and a small child. We were warm with greetings and it was an exciting experience to see them again. Siri looked very fit, tanned and healthy. She was dressed in a colourful blouse and mini-skirt and looked almost like a native girl. They said that the male child had been adopted by them in Brookland on recommendation of Casel's mother Kate Poute. His name was René.

When I asked what the strange sound was that filled the air with a cheerful merriment, Casel explained that this was the singing trees from Oberon. He pointed to some large trees which had orange leaves and branches that hung down like a willow's, but wavered in the breeze.

"The leaves are fluted and catch the breeze, and this produces that sound which we enjoy throughout the Pacific region; wherever there are fish people there are their singing trees," Casel said.

I was amazed, amused and expectant of further wonders as we drove to their house in an inner part of Phoenix City.

117

I had a relatively normal evening with Casel, Siri and René. It was a mixture of becoming familiar with them again and hearing all the news of the Pacific.

I learnt that the fish people now numbered several hundred thousand and were equally distributed throughout the three basin zones. They had already taken on many tasks related to fish farming and had introduced fish creatures from their own planet for farming. Fish people were also participating in some of the deep sea mining facility construction and investigation of reserves of minerals.

Casel had met many fish people and said that they were a little frightening at first as any quite unusual creature is at first sight. However they were friendly, cheerful and learnt quickly to read maps and followed instructions in the form of diagrams. They could also easily mimic human actions in the operation of machinery and were invaluable for the deepest part of the trenches of the Pacific. Within ten years it was expected that their numbers would be in the millions and they would be a great resource for the development of the Pacific region.

I was as yet unprepared for the sociable human-like way the fish people associated amongst themselves. How quickly they had adapted and how resourceful they had been at producing necessary food and medicinal items for themselves from their stock of Oberon gametes of fishes and plants.

The whole time on Phoenix Island I was to experience the harmonious sounds of the singing trees. This sound never ceased and was to become a famous tourist attraction in itself. I was delighted and slept ever so well in the warm night air filled with the sound of the singing trees.

My anticipation was high as Casel drove us to the harbour of Phoenix Island. I had some idea what a fish looks like in their various forms but I just couldn't imagine a fish person. I wanted to see them with my own eyes and perhaps we could communicate in some way, some sub-conscious symbolism might pass between us. Perhaps they could come to know that I was also from Oberon although coming to Earth in a completely different way. No matter was transported to Earth when I came here only psychic energy; only a force field of semi-conscious being; a being that I only truly knew on planet Oberon, and was not manifest to me or any human on Earth.

We, Casel and I, sped along swiftly in the small ex-US Navy frigate that travelled daily to the island of the fish people. The sea was calm and we watched the stream of wave that spread out from the bow of the boat. All was quiet. There were no singing trees.

Then we went downstairs to a lounge area where Casel spread a map on a low table. He pointed out the three basins with which I was familiar and the three islands of Mariana, Phoenix and Tonga. Then he showed me the location of the three islands which were almost completely inhabited by fish people, Oberon North, South, and Central. He explained that there were human advisers on these islands. He also said that it was from these islands that the main islands had gotten reports of disappearances of working advisers from about six months ago.

My role was to find out what the fish people knew about these disappearances and what could be done to prevent any re-occurrence of these shocking events. Casel did not know how I could find out but he understood that I had some special relation to these alien creatures. He knew that I had received personal messages from Oberon. No other human could as yet hold any kind of revealing dialogue with the fish people. It was therefore entirely up to me to solve this problem and save Global Monarch from future embarrassment.

Casel was a self-assured young man, he felt he knew what was important; the interests of Global Monarch. The loss of life didn't seem too significant to him nor the implications for the fish people who were immediately cast under suspicion. The loss of life on this scale and frequency, I felt was extremely sad. The fact that the fish people could be suspected of misconduct, conduct suggesting that they could not now or perhaps ever be trusted was a bazaar circumstance of mere co-incidence. It was this suspicion which I soon hoped to prove false.

I wished with all my human heart to dispel any bad feeling towards the fish people and clear their name. The next few days would be crucial to their continued existence; to being seen as compatible with humans.

We saw the island of Oberon Central in the distance, a wide expanse of low hills with an orange colour. We sped closer and I could soon hear the singing trees. It was a magical sound, a drone, a hum, a whistle, like a wind-chime only with the notes elongated and rising and falling but continuously wearing a melody of a thousand voices.

The sound of the singing trees grew louder as we drew closer to the island. Then I could see that we were drawing near to a dock.

On the dock stood two human-like forms, grey in colour. As we stopped beside the dock I knew that these were fish people. They were short, between three or four metres high. Yes, they had arms and legs and fingers on their hands. They stared with big fish eyes. Their heads were poking down, lowered. They were scaly creatures, one was orange in colour on the bottom half and the other yellow. They both had two fins on either side where a human's hips would be.

We stepped off the boat onto the dock and the two figures stepped forward. They first greeted Casel by raising their arms and putting their hands on his shoulders. Then they did the same to me.

We stood awkwardly for about a minute and then they looked at each other making small squealing sounds. They waved their arms slowly as if offering their island to us and welcoming us to their home.

Then they gestured us forward along the dock to the shore. We walked behind them up a rough path to a low building made of the boron/mercury material. We followed them through a low doorway into a kind of bar. It had been built by humans for them and did indeed resemble a typical bar-room. There were tables and chairs around which sat about twenty fish people. A long bar with stools was along one wall where another five fish people sat. They were eating and drinking just like humans would but there were high pitched sounds made by the fish people as they spoke to each other.

We; Casel, I and the two fish people sat down at a table and one fish person brought drinks. This particular one was just like a waiter; he wiped the table top and left four green drinks in glasses. Casel said that usually the drinks of the fish people were undrinkable by humans but the food that they ate was quite tasty. I tried my drink and it just tasted like salty seaweed, not appetizing at all. Casel could tell I was not enjoying it so he pointed to a coke machine by a nearby wall. The nearest fish person of the two picked up two tokens from a bowl on the table, went to the coke machine and got Casel and myself a coke each.

I was uneasy in this environment, the sights and sounds of the fish people were too unusual. I sipped my coke and Casel did the same with his. The two fish people sipped their drinks. The fish-waiter returned with two plates of food. It looked quite good, apparently some fish had been wrapped in sea-weed and steamed. The waiter waited, looking around the table. Then it went and came back with knives and forks and placed them on the table. We ate the food which was very good, it had some strong savoury flavour. The fish was unlike any I had previously eaten. It was more fleshy, more like chicken only with a yellow tinge.

At that point I saw a group of fish people get up onto a stage at one end of the room. They picked up various objects and adjusted what seemed to be micro-phones. They all stood with their objects and one held a micro-phone in it's hand. I deduced that I was to experience some kind of performance. Then the fish-group started making sounds on the objects. It was fish music and each fish-player had a kind of marine instrument to make sounds on. Two of the fish group held conches, one was small the other quite large. Two others had stringed instruments made of threads of seaweed stretched across big orange gourds. A fifth fish person held a percussion instrument, a type of tambourine or drum.

They played rhythmically and fast and it was quite musical until the singer made high sounding grunts and squeals into the micro-phone which amplified it's voice. One conch had a low bass sound, the other a higher whistling sound and the singer was somewhere between them in pitch, elongating the sound and waving it's arms.

I was quite awestruck with this display, it was similar to a musical band of humans but to hear the sounds and see the fish group perform was completely amazing. The music stopped after an hour and the fish musicians stepped down from the stage as their audience applauded them, clapping and squealing in a very enthusiastic way.

We sat for another quarter of an hour then Casel said we may as well leave the bar. Casel and I stood, the two fish people at our table also stood. Casel waved towards the door indicating that we were going to leave. The two fish persons bowed to us and waved their arms as they looked from us towards other tables where the fish people were staring at us. They all had strange leering, wide smiles.

Casel and I walked out of the low door and into the brightness of spring sunshine, warm, with a cool breeze.

120

Later that evening I spoke with Casel at the house of a managing adviser. Casel ruminated cheerfully-

"I've watched these fish people when they work and when they are at leisure. They seem quite innocent and child-like, you can tell when they laugh, a kind of muffled chuckling squeal and they hold their heads up. Also you have some surprises when you see them in the other zones, I hope you get to the other zones. I won't tell you but the fish people are taking to our ways very well. But for the life of me I can't tell the difference between the males and the females, they say orange bodied ones are the males and the ones with yellow bodies are the females."

Casel laughed heartily. I couldn't tell the difference either; they all looked the same to me, except for their height which I supposed reflected their age.

120

Later that evening I spoke with Casel at the house of a managing adviser. Casel ruminated cheerfully-

"I've watched these fish people when they work and when they are at leisure. They seem quite innocent and child-like, you can tell when they laugh, a kind of muffled chuckling squeal and they hold their heads up. Also you have some surprises when you see them in the other zones; I hope you get to the other zones. I won't tell you but the fish people are taking to our ways very well. But for the life of me I can't tell the difference between the males and the females, they say orange bodied ones are the males and the ones with yellow bodies are the females."

Casel laughed heartily. I couldn't tell the difference either; they all looked the same to me, except for their height which I supposed reflected their age.

121

The next morning an adviser took me to a low building which had frangipani trees growing around it.

We entered and he explained that this is where he instructed several representatives of the fish people. He showed me a shelf of maps, a large collection of photographs, another shelf containing diagrams and samples of rocks. A large table had compasses, depth reading equipment, radar and various other types of electrical equipment.

The adviser took an hour to show me around and then two fish persons made sounds by rubbing their hands on the door. The adviser let them in and I was again in the presence of these, my fellow beings, the fish persons from planet Oberon.

One of the fish persons went immediately to an album of photos of earth fishes and found a picture of a shark. Next it found photos of marine plant varieties from planet Oberon. It placed the two photos together and smiled and waved its hands. There was obviously a connection between the sharks and a plant specie photograph had he selected from the plant album.

The adviser said that the fish people had been working on a deterrent chemical derived from this plant, to keep the sharks away from humans and fish people. The adviser knew exactly why I was visiting the island and produced an album of newspaper cuttings. He turned to a page showing pictures and articles of the disappearances of human adviser workers. Then he pointed to photos of the missing men and a map showing where they had disappeared.

The fish person who had shown us the shark photos got the album of Oberon plants, pointed to one particular plant and put it beside the articles on the missing advisers. Then it did a strange thing; it lifted my arm and seemed to be pretending to eat it by opening and closing its mouth and showing it's teeth close to my arm. It was obvious, the fish people or some fish people found human flesh edible. Then this fish creature held out its arms and waved them conversely and horizontally, it also nodded emphatically. It seemed to be indicating that this liking for human flesh would end. It pointed to the photos of the sharks and the plant that was connected with them, then it pointed to the photos of the missing advisers and indicated that the other plant was connected with these.

The message was clear to me. The first Oberon plant deterred sharks from attacking humans and the second plant had the quality of deterring fish people from a liking of human flesh.

I felt relieved looked into the fish creature's large eyes, which had huge black pupils surrounded by a thick ring of green with sparkles of yellow flashing.

Next the fish person got out a map and pointed, with a partially webbed finger, to the island of Mariana. Then it got out a book of agendas and calendars and indicated a date, two days in the future. It then put its hands on my shoulders and looked into my face. After a short time it stood back pointed to me, the island on the map and the date on the calendar. The fish person squealed in a pleased manner and waved towards its companion who waved its hand in return and also squealed and grunted a few times.

Then they left and I faced the adviser who did not seem surprised, apparently he was used to the fish people or maybe just these two particular ones. I said what I was thinking, that the fish creature had been trying to say that I should go to Mariana Island, Northern zone on the date, two days from now. He agreed that that was what the fish person was saying and we both sighed to find we knew or thought we knew we had some clue as to a solution to our mutual problem.

122

I must say, I had the horrors. I felt as though I could not speak to anyone about what I had heard and seen that day. That night I had intensely vivid nightmares, the first bad dreams I had had as a human. I dreamt of an under-water environment; of sharks, fish people and humans in a fearful struggle of life and death. I dreamt of human advisers in their faun uniforms falling into the ocean and being ripped apart by fearsome sharks and fish people.

I awoke in a sweat of fear, shaken and exhausted. I had a shower and felt a little better. That day I could not bring myself to tell Casel what had happened other than that I was going to Mariana island within two days.

123

I left Phoenix island with mixed feelings the next day. I took a jet from the airport and was wished goodbye by a group of about twenty fish people who waved, squealed and grunted. Casel, Siri and a number of advisers also said goodbye, wishing me good luck and good weather.

I arrived at Mariana Island six hours later that same day. As I stepped down the gangway I heard without listening the sound of singing trees. It was dusk and there was a brilliant sunset and it was very humid. As I descended I saw Spin and a young woman at his side that I recognised as Pamela. At their feet stood a small child who I guessed was Rubin their son, and Randy's grandson.

Then ensued a similar scene as had occurred on Phoenix island, I went to Spin's house and we talked about life on the island and of fish people. Pamela also informed me of the latest developments with TriStar, how they had designed models for the three regional basins and how these were now, with the help of the fish people, being put into place.

I had a good sleep that night and was ready the next morning for any meetings with fish people that might eventuate. I had a similar meal as on Phoenix island at a bar-room with Spin and Pamela, there was no music this time. After this event we walked to the beach where to my surprise I saw a game of European football played by fish people on the beach. About two hundred fish people were lying in the shallows of the water watching the game and they cheered, squealing in high pitched voices when a goal was scored. Then there was a game of volleyball with the fish players leaping and groaning in the hot humid air.

It was late in the afternoon when an adviser manager took me to a work area on Oberon North Island.

Here were large vats for refining plant material and pipes shifting chemicals to storage areas. Several fish persons approached us and we went with them to a similar information shelter as on Oberon Central Island where there were books and videos and electrical equipment.

The adviser took down an album filled with newspaper cuttings and as had happened on Oberon Central Island pointed to cuttings of articles on the missing advisers. One of the fish persons went to a cupboard near the window and opening it took down a five-litre container of a liquid and some diagrams and formulas on sheets of paper. It placed these beside the album of newspaper cuttings and grunted, as if to say, there, that's your deterrent chemical. Yes, it seemed that the fish people had refined a chemical that could stop themselves liking human flesh.

Then this fish person got out a folder of photos and found a photo of sharks. It placed this beside the album of newspaper cuttings. It pointed at the liquid in the container and raised one finger and then pointed, first at the album and then at the photos of sharks, then it raised two fingers. The meaning of this was not at first obvious but then the fish person put one hand on the container and another on the album and folder. It let out a long grunting sigh and nodded.

This time it was definite what the fish person meant. The one deterrent chemical had the ability of keeping both sharks and fish people away from humans. I knew their manners now so I bowed and waved my hands and was greeted by a similar response of agreement by the fish person.

I took a fast boat back to the main island of Mariana and retired to Spin's house. It was a great family gathering with young Rubin who was about four years old. We talked late into the night and I then slept much better as the singing trees played their cheerful tune.

124

The next morning Spin took me to see a managing adviser and I handed over the container of liquid and the folder of diagrams and formulas. I supposed some chemical synthesis could be made and this chemical could be manufactured in large quantities. No doubt there were some chemicals existing on planet Oberon that were only recently introduced to the oceans of Earth but I still held hopes of success.

I told Spin that the fish people had invented a chemical that could deter sharks from attacking humans. Spin felt that this called for some celebration that would be good for publicity on the islands; he therefore took me to meet a group of fish people and had our photo taken shaking hands with them.

One of the fish people stepped forward after the photo was taken and produced a photograph of the annual display of pyrotechnics on the island. It then did a strange thing. Joining arms with a group of ten fish people they formed a circle and put their heads close together. They made a sound like a drone rising ever louder, then raised their arms up towards the sky.

I did not know what to make of this and only looked puzzled at them when they finally ceased and turned to face me. The fish person with the photo of the fireworks held up the photo and pointed with a long index finger to it. It then grunted and waved its arms up and down. I remained puzzled and so I bowed and shook hands with this fish person.

The rest of the day passed with a tour of the island with Spin and Pamela. Throughout these days I enjoyed the entrancing hum and drone of the singing trees. I settled down to sleep that night feeling that things had improved and that the fish people who had horrified me with their gruesome liking for human flesh had redeemed themselves.

125

I seemed to sleep very well, not waking once, but once I did wake I had a feeling that I had resolved something in my sleep.

Gradually a few pieces of dreams came together in my head and I remembered that the fish persons once could produce apparitions above the oceans of Oberon. In my mind this fact seemed to be linked to the photograph of fireworks and the ritual performance of the fish people the day before.

When I told Spin about this ability of the fish people he agreed that there was some connection between these events. We therefore went back to the same group of fish people and indicated that we were interested in their performance and the fireworks. One of them produced a diary which had symbols scrawled in its columns. The fish person pointed as was their means of communicating to a date, the next week. Next it took out a map from a Hessian bag it was carrying and again pointed to, this time, Tonga Island in the South Pacific. The fish person placed both it's hands on my shoulders and squealed several times, stepped back, pointed again to the island on the map and then to the date in the diary.

Spin and I agreed that the fish person wanted me to witness the conjuring of an apparition on this day, on this island. I was pleased that we could communicate with these fish creatures and that I, maybe soon, would be able to see the creation of one of their apparitions.

I thought about this for the rest of the day and decided that I would like it if Miriam too could see the apparition. I therefore phoned Miriam and asked her if she could fly out to Tonga Island by the date specified. She said she would try to book a flight the next morning.

126

I stayed two more days on Mariana Island and then caught a jet to Tonga Island in the South Pacific region. It was a long trip, fourteen hours and I was glad to step off the plane and drive in a taxi to a Hotel. The incessant sound of the singing trees wafted in the cool air.

It was five days until the date set aside for the witnessing of the apparition. I went swimming on a deserted beach bordered by palm trees and singing trees. I had a call from Miriam the second day, she was leaving home that day and would be on Tonga Island the following morning.

A manager from Pacific Trust who had actually been appointed by Stanley Poute showed me around the island and I met some of the native people.

The next morning I went to the airport to meet the plane that Miriam would be on and greeted her as she stepped down from it. We hugged and walked to the passenger lounge where we had coffee and chatted about every little detail that had occurred. She was excitedly expectant about meeting a fish person so that afternoon we went on a boat to Oberon South Island where there were fish people.

We were greeted at the dock by a group of six fish people. Miriam stood well back from them and seemed to be taking their appearance well into consideration. Each one of them however went through the manner of greeting that was peculiarly theirs. They one by one stepped close, first to me and then Miriam and placed a hand on each shoulder. This done there was a round of squealing, grunting and waving of hands. Then one of them shook hands with me, I don't know why, and gestured to a low building along the beach and back under the trees.

We followed the group to this building where once inside one fish person waved at some pictures on the wall with its hand. The large pictures were of pyrotechnics which seemed to be particularly attractive to fish people. I thought that perhaps this had some connection with the apparitions. The fish people seemed to know me wherever I went and what I was there for.

One of the fish persons started gesturing. It placed a hand on a glass jug on a table containing a green liquid and then each fish person pointed to their head and then pointed upwards, waving their hands. Then the fish person nodded indicating a "no" signal but quickly pointed to the jug and to me and nodded again as if to say "yes".

I wasn't exactly sure what it meant but then it poured a glass-full of the liquid and indicated that I should drink it. I meaning to comply reached for the glass but then the fish person waved its arms horizontally and nodded "no". I was confused but the fish creature pointed to a date on a calendar on the wall. It was the date when I was to see the apparition. I still wasn't sure what the creature had meant but I smiled pleasantly and the fish person grunted and the other fish people squealed amongst themselves.

71

This over with, apparently, we, Miriam and I and two of the fish people, went to yet another bar room where Miriam was as surprised as I had been to see fish people sitting, drinking, eating and chatting like humans. Miriam and I were served a meal of grilled fish and some strange yellow marine vegetable which was quite tasty. I advised her to have a coke to accompany the meal and we sat back sipping our cokes as the two fish persons looked around them at other tables where fish people were sitting, some of them couldn't help staring at us with their big unblinking eyes.

127

Late that afternoon Miriam and I returned to the hotel and we were having coffees. I brought some newspapers from a table where they were kept for guests. We were browsing through the local news when I, reading the New York Times turned to page three. There I saw a picture of myself and a group of fish people. The headline read: ALIEN FISH PEOPLE DISCOVER SHARK DETERRENT.

I went on reading about the resourcefulness of the fish people and their innate intelligence. The article said that the fish people were collaborating with Global Monarch for purposes of mining, fish farming and tourism. The article also said that I, Randolph Bilder was managing director of the Global Monarch subsidiary Pacific Trust Pty. Ltd.

I showed Miriam the article and she was very pleased, especially now that I was becoming famous.

128

We retired early to our room and chatted idly for several hours. Thick grey clouds were sweeping in on the western horizon. That night there was a storm that worsened and lasted through the following morning. It was a fierce storm at its worst with strong winds, heavy rain and thunder and lightening.

When the storm subsided about lunch time Miriam and I went to the beach where trees had been uprooted and roofs of buildings had been blown away. We met a group of fish people who greeted us in their normal fashion and then began to perform some rituals.

They formed circles of about ten or twelve of them, linking arms, chanting in grunts and squeals and then raised their hands up to the sky.

One fish person produced a bottle of green liquid and a glass, from this they all drank and then the fish person offered me some. I did not want to appear unfriendly so I had a few mouthfuls. Although it didn't taste too bad it was still a strange concoction; salty and like sea-weed in a thick kind of way. I didn't notice anything at first. The fish people produced some of their musical instruments, conches and drums and played on them while chanting. Gradually in the sky above us a yellow haze formed, then there was a lightening flash and thunder.

I began to feel highly elated and felt pins and needles in my body especially a tingling sensation at the temples. I watched the sky as the colour deepened and a haze spread to the horizon. Then at the seeming centre of the yellow haze a glistening orb formed, and then others of various sizes. At cloud level the orbs spread rapidly, glistening and glowing like huge bubbles.

The fish people were very excited and began to dance. I felt extremely happy and my awareness expanded cosmically until I felt at one with the whole universe. I also felt that I was as old as the universe, infinitely old and infinitely wise.

In this all knowing state I became aware of many things one of which was that the boy child René, the adopted son of Casel and Siri was my child, mine and Kate Poute's child. I had a premonition that he would be like Mia, a lover of the waters, and would have a special affinity with the fish people.

The air was thick, it seemed denser to me, full of pulsating vibrations emanating from the yellow orbs in the sky. These vibrations penetrated my mind and connected me subconsciously with the group of fish people surrounding me. They were stomping wildly into the sand and waving their arms. At that point I wanted to join them. I knew that this was not just a common apparition that the fish people, with my help and the help of the liquid I had drunk, had conjured up.

These orbs in the sky were the spirit beings, the cloud people of Oberon, they had arrived. And the sky was yellow and the sea reflected a deep orange glow. And the fish people raised their scaly heads and laughed for joy.

129

These were strange days.

Fortunately for everyone my strangeness was not to last for long. The cloud people were now established over the oceans of planet Earth their presence casting a warm glow throughout the skies and enabling the fish people to now make their rituals, drink their magic drink, and create the apparitions.

That night I went to sleep feeling a great sense of tiredness and relief. I awoke in the middle of the night feeling very strange. My skin seemed tight on my body and when I touched it felt like leather. I had a tingling sensation in my brain. Somehow between the drink that the fish people had given to me and the coming of the spirit beings I had been affected, permanently, irretrievably. I went back to sleep. It was a restless sleep with much tossing and turning.

130

In the early morning light I dozed. The light that came through the window seemed to have an orange glow, a shimmering presence that hung in the air and calmed me while it yet excited me.

I went into the bathroom to have a shower. I removed my pyjamas. I looked down at my body. It had changed during the night. It was a yellowish colour with bruises, dark patches of skin. I looked into the mirror. My face seemed strange, more elongated, the eyes bigger than usual. Perhaps, I thought, I was having a hangover from drinking the fish people's brew.

I turned on the shower and stepped under the stream of hot water. The feeling of water on my skin was thrilling like going for a swim in a hot swimming pool. I stayed for a long time, the water beating down and flowing over me. I felt a further tightening of my skin, a kind of crawling, itchy sensation. I looked at my arms and legs which seemed thinner than usual and then as I looked further over my body I noticed grooves forming in the skin. At first lines on my skin darkened , then the skin separated and began to form into scales.

Strangeness affected my head and brain, I felt them moving and changing shape.

The water beat down and flowed in streams to the floor of the shower cubicle. I stayed for an hour. I stayed there for two hours, fascinated, feeling slight pains but mostly an elation; a feeling of release.

I looked at my hands and toes which had lengthened and now looked like a fish person's. I felt my chest swell and stretch, growing as the waters flowed down. I put my hands up to my face and felt the large mouth and sharpened teeth, the bulging eyes and the changed shape of my skull.

I stepped out of the shower and looked into the mirror. I had the body of a fish person. I moved part of my body where my neck would normally be thinner. I moved two areas of my neck area and realized that these were gills through which I would be able to breathe under water. I was without the fins which usually protruded from the hip area of a fish person. I touched my chest and lower body; it was slippery to my touch, the scales slightly blue in colour. I was orange in the lower part of my body. I knew then that I would never again play at being a human.

I then thought of Miriam and not wanting to disturb her I crept into the bedroom intending to slip out of the door without rousing her. But she heard me, she stirred, she raised herself in the bed and stared gasping at me.

I stepped to the bedside cupboard and collected my watch and a gold chain that Randolph Bilder normally wore around his neck. I put these on. Miriam looked at me, she understood. I the fish person with her husband's body was now completely a fish person. She held her hands to her mouth.

"Randy!" she cried. "Where is my Randy?"

I raised my arms in puzzlement and moved uneasily about the room. I looked out of the window of the hotel. I could see the beach front. I felt a sudden longing to be in the ocean, to be in my natural environment, to be truly myself. I pointed out the window at the sea.

Miriam rose from the bed and also looked out the window at where I pointed with a long scaly webbed fish finger. I made a movement as if diving into water. Miriam understood. She quickly dressed.

We went out of the apartment to the lift. She could only star at me as we waited. The lift came. We entered. I looked at myself in the lift mirror. I was shorter than Miriam. I was wearing a human's watch and I had a gold chain around my thick neck. We stepped out into the large uninhabited lobby of the hotel and then out the front doors. We were walking along the street, there were few people, but they stopped and stared at us. We walked down a ramp onto the deserted beach and then to the water's edge. I put my two hands on Miriam's shoulders as a final gesture then turned to enter the waters. Miriam stopped me and removed the watch and gold chain. Then I strode through the shallows and low breaking waves.

As I stepped I saw a figure rising from out of the ocean, first the head, then the shoulders, chest and arms. It was a human. As I waded closer and deeper I saw that the figure was Randolph Bilder the human that I had once been. I as myself, my body as it had been yesterday and every day for the last three and a half months.

Randolph Bilder passed me with a knowing stare. Then I noticed that he had fins where his hips were and I knew that he also had been transformed overnight; but from a fish person into a human being.

As I looked back over my shoulder I saw the naked body, with fins, striding through the low breakwater. Miriam was running and embraced him. They stood still for a few minutes then Miriam put his watch on his arm and the gold chain around his neck ... they kissed again. I turned towards the ocean and plunged deep into its comforting encompassment.

131

"Hello, this is Randolph Bilder otherwise known as Randy Bilder. I have discovered the manuscript journals of Mr. Alien, the notorious Alien X. I am going to finish the last few pages, for whom it may concern; for Miriam and me, for Mr. Alien, for all humans, for all fish people, for posterity.

It's just like Oberon, I think, here are the cloud people with whom I am now able to communicate telepathically. Here is their shimmering orange glow over the waters and here are the fish people, living, working and becoming just another feature of this part of the universe. It is a part of the universe that has not previously known fish people or spirit beings. But it is a lucky planet, a planet of hope, joy and sharing of its wonders.

132

I was aware, don't ask me how, that I was to see apparitions that day. Apparitions such as I had seen on planet Oberon.

Miriam and I knew this. We prepared ourselves by having a fine lunch in the hotel restaurant. My fins had retracted, disappeared and though a slight bruise was still evident no-one would ever know when they saw me once more in my human's clothes.

We took a large sailing boat out to Oberon South Island and we were greeted by a group of fish people. They took us to a beach not far from the dock where hundreds of fish people were laying on the sand and frolicking in the shallows. We watched them for more than an hour, then a group of them came forward, some of them took out instruments;

conches, stringed gourds and a drum. They began to play their music. Another group of about thirty fish people formed circles and linked arms and began to chant, grunting and squealing. This went on for another hour, then a number of them separated, took out some glass bottles and glasses from Hessian bags and poured drinks of a bright reddish colour. They passed these around and sipped and squealed excitedly.

After much waving of arms, the music quickened its tempo. The fish people formed circles again, yelped and let out elongated droning sounds. Each of them raised their arms up towards the sky and waved their hands.

Then they all sat as Miriam and I was sitting and looked out above the ocean. A bright clear light formed above the waters, almost touching the water. This light glistened with crystalline forms and was forever changing. I thought it was the most wonderful thing I had ever seen. The fish people let out sighs of enjoyment and pleasure. The apparition took on multi-coloured hues, and it evolved in multi-facets, shimmering in the air.

Miriam was very pleased with the apparition and with me. She smiled as I remembered her smiling, when great happiness filled her with mirth and joy.

As we sailed back to the main island I noticed that the singing trees could not be heard out here on the water. I looked up to the sky where clusters of cloud people were hovering; where they would be suspended for all time.

We stepped down from the boat onto a wharf. I turned to Miriam, I smiled. I said, "OK that's it. Book the tickets, let's go home."

"Yes," she replied, "let's go home."

133

We took the early morning flight at Tonga airport two days later. To tell the truth I never have felt so fresh, so complete, so tranquil.

I looked at Miriam and smiled. Then I looked into a mirror at my face. I laughed. I couldn't believe that mischievous glint in *my* eyes.

Zeitfracht Medien GmbH
Ferdinand-Jühlke-Straße 7
99095 Erfurt, Deutschland
produktsicherheit@kolibri360.de

Druck:
CPI Druckdienstleistungen GmbH
im Auftrag der
Zeitfracht Medien GmbH
Ein Unternehmen der Zeitfracht - Gruppe
Ferdinand-Jühlke-Str. 7
99095 Erfurt